This is not smart.

Ha. That was an understatement.

He'd brought the reason for his fall from Heaven to his personal home, the one place no one else—neither human nor otherworldly being—knew about.

Not smart.

Neither is still holding on to her.

The sharp thought slid through his mind, and he pulled his arms from Billie's body. Took a step away from her.

She regarded him for a long moment, expression unreadable.

Her fear hung on the air, tainted it. As did her anger. And something far more raw and primitive. The very thing he'd been able to tap into when he'd influenced her to kiss him.

Desire.

It threaded around him, tendrils and wisps of an emotion he had little defense against.

Bringing her here was not smart at all.

LEXXIE COUPER

DESTINY'S KNIGHT

GUARDED SOULS Book 1

LexxieCouper.com

Guarded Souls Series

Book 1: Destiny's Knight
Book 2: Hope's Wish
Book 3: Amber's Heat

Dedication

For those out there who have fallen and got back up again.

Chapter One

"Don't open your door."

Billie Sheridan frowned at the fierce terror in her agent's voice. There'd been no greeting, no apology for waking her at 2:45 am, just that one terse command drenched in fear cutting through the fog of Billie's disturbed sleep.

Don't open your door.

Shoving the heavy waves of her hair—currently dyed a copper auburn and messy as all hell from sleep—from her face, she wriggled into an upright position on her bed. "What the hell are you talking about, Adelaide?"

"They've lost him," Adelaide Williams rasped through the cellphone connection, a lifetime of cigarettes roughening her voice. "He slipped his ankle restraint a day ago. The police have no idea where he is."

Billie frowned again. "Addy, I have no idea

who you're talking about. Are you sure you have the right client?"

"Christ on a fucking pony, I knew this was going to come back and bite me on the ass," Adelaide muttered.

Billie blinked. Adelaide never cursed. The woman was a paragon of good manners.

A sharp sigh blew into the phone, loud enough to distort in Billie's ear. "Honey," Adelaide went on, her voice calmer but no less husky. "I have something to tell you, and I need you to not freak out, okay?"

Billie shifted on the bed until she was cross-legged, a disquieting knot making itself at home in her stomach.

Adelaide Williams had been her agent from the day she'd been cast as Destiny Blaq, demon assassin extraordinaire. Not once in all those years had she ever told Billie to not freak out—not even when the studio tried to enforce a clause in her contract that demanded she go topless for an entire episode.

Brief glimpses of full-frontal nudity were so passé now. In today's cutthroat world of streaming and cable TV, forty-five *minutes* of nudity was the way to go, a sure-fire path to ratings success.

Thank God Adelaide had nixed that mandate quick smart. No freaking out required on Billie's behalf. A flash of side-boob here and there was okay, but strutting about on set topless, fighting demons that way…yeah, Billie would quit before that happened. Adelaide knew it. So did almost everyone who worked on *Destiny's Knight*, from the showrunner right down to the key grip.

So what possible situation could make Adelaide sound so frazzled now?

"Promise me you won't freak out, B," Adelaide demanded.

Billie huffed out a shallow breath as she rubbed at her arm. "I won't freak out, Addy. I promise. Now tell me what's going on."

Adelaide let out a sigh far more shaky than her previous one. "Two months ago, the authorities arrested a man who had been stalking you. He was convinced he was the embodiment of Wraif and was determined to reclaim you—and by *you*, I mean Destiny. He's a whack job, honey; he's dangerous and he's obsessed with you."

A prickling tension crawled up Billie's spine and over her scalp.

Wraif was her character's arch nemesis, a lust demon who used pleasure to kill his victims, and who'd been Destiny's lover in the pilot episode. Wraif's fall from Destiny's bed came when he seduced her twin sister to her death in retaliation for Destiny refusing to let him dominate her via BDSM games. Every time Wraif appeared in a story arc, the ratings spiked—the audience loved his deranged, psychotic obsession, and Destiny's hatred of him.

The actor who played Wraif was a born sweetie with a wife and brood of children. Definitely the antithesis of his character on the show.

Anyone who believed themselves to be Wraif would need to be unhinged.

A cold shiver joined the prickling heat creeping over Billie. Unhinged, obsessed with her, and on the loose, it seemed. Not a good combination.

She swallowed. "Why do I not know anything about this?"

Adelaide made a frustrated sound. Or maybe an embarrassed one. "He'd sent over fifty letters to the studio before the CEO contacted the police. By the time they caught him, he'd sent fifty more, each more graphic than the last about his plans for you." She paused, the heavy silence broken by the hammering thump of Billie's heart in her ears. "Once they caught him, I didn't think you needed to be worried. The authorities had him. He was going to jail. You didn't need to be…"

"Freaked out?" Billie finished for her. Her heart wasn't just thumping in her ears now; it was doing its damnedest to hammer its way out of her body.

Adelaide had the good grace to mutter out an apologetic sound that turned into an apologetic cough. "I'm sorry, hon. But the Golden Globes were only a week away and I made the call. I didn't think he'd get away."

Billie closed her eyes and exhaled slowly. "But he has?"

"Yes."

"And he's coming for me?"

"The authorities believe so."

"Awesome."

Adelaide made another one of those ambiguous grunts: part shame, part frustration. It was a noise Billie would gladly like to never hear her make again. It was so out of character for her.

Adelaide had swooped into the waiting area of the *Destiny's Knight* open-call audition—an audition Billie had only attended as support for her roommate, the only real friend she'd made since moving to the US. Addy had thrust her card into Billie's hand and proceeded to sweet-talk the casting director into letting her read for the role of Destiny.

Up until that point, the sum total of acting work Billie had done was in a dog shampoo commercial back home in Australia, and she'd only landed that gig because she'd been best friends with the advertising agency's creative director's daughter.

Of course, her roommate stopped talking to her the day she was cast as Destiny, something that still hurt Billie deeply. Just as she'd been hurt when her best friend stopped talking to her over the dog shampoo commercial. For Pete's sake, Billie hadn't been upset when Jenny passed her black-belt ranking on the same day Billie had failed.

So much for best friends through thick and thin.

Adelaide was the closest thing Billie had to a BFF now, which was kind of sad if she thought about it. But the agent had stood by her no matter what, even during the first season of *Destiny's Knight*, when the critics slammed Billie for being a "talentless nobody thrust into an underserved limelight."

In the four years since, as the show became a ratings juggernaut and cult phenomenon, and Billie's acting talent was lauded as "ethereal" and "mesmerizing," Adelaide had become more and more an integral part of Billie's life. The non-judgmental mother she never had.

"Just don't open the door to anyone," Adelaide repeated, stress eating into the instruction. "The cops are sending over a detail now. When they get there, I'll let you know. Plus, I've arranged extra protection for you with—"

A sharp buzz sliced across Adelaide's words.

Billie jumped, dropping her phone in the process and letting out a little squeak her kick-ass character would have been completely embarrassed by.

"Billie?" her agent's voice—tinny and faint—wafted up from the mattress.

The buzz came again, sharp and insistent.

Someone was at the front gate of her home, pressing the intercom button.

"Billie?"

Billie's heart crashed fast in her throat.

The intercom buzzed again. Longer this time.

Billie stared through her bedroom's open door at the darkness of her home beyond. A weak silver glow touched the edges and surfaces of her furniture, the moon outside barely penetrating her living room through the floor-to-ceiling glass doors that opened out onto the ocean-facing balcony.

"Billie?"

She started, Adelaide's distant voice like a scream in the silence.

The gate buzzer sawed at the darkness once more.

Snatching up her phone, she raised it to her ear. "There's someone here."

"Don't open the door!" Adelaide damn near screeched. "The cops shouldn't be there yet. Or the guy from the security agency."

Billie stared into the gloom beyond her bedroom door. "But what if they are?"

"I...I don't know," Adelaide admitted, the confession becoming a wheezy cough. If Billie hadn't been so on edge, she would have been gobsmacked. Adelaide Williams *never* admitted to not knowing something.

For a fifth time, her intercom buzzed. Loud. Long. Impatient.

"I'll go see who it is," Billie said, beginning to climb off her bed.

"No!" Adelaide burst out. "If it's Gilbert, he'll know you're home."

Billie paused on the edge of her bed. "My stalker's name is Gilbert?" A giggling snort escaped her. "Well, that's just a ridiculous name for a stalker."

"Billie," Adelaide snapped.

"Sorry." Billie blushed. A lifetime of being raised by a strict Protestant mother had conditioned her to be shamed by admonishment.

Once again, the intercom buzzed.

"I'm going to answer it," she announced, scrambling completely off the bed. Ignoring her robe, she hurried from her bedroom into the darkness of her home.

"Wilhelmina Sheridan, don't you dare!"

Billie had a moment to register her agent

had resorted to using her full name, just like a mother would a naughty child in need of reprimand, before guilt made her aware of the panic in Adelaide's voice.

But guilt wasn't enough to stop her from hurrying to the intercom panel. If nothing else, she wanted to see what a stalker called Gilbert looked like—if it was indeed Gilbert pressing the button on the other side of her locked gate.

"It's okay," she muttered into her phone as she approached the entry foyer. "Whoever it is, they can't get in. I've got a state-of-the-art security system, remember."

The buzzer drowned out Adelaide's response.

Heart thumping, she jabbed at the button beside the comm-link and activated the CCTV camera positioned above the security panel at her gate.

She had to see whoever it was before she said anything.

The small black screen in the control panel instantly filled with a full-color image of the man purporting to be from Guarded Souls Security and Protection.

A shiver ran up Billie's spine, turning her nipples hard. Her lips parted in a soft gasp. The junction of her thighs throbbed.

He was tall. Tall and broad-shouldered and lean-hipped. The faded jeans and black leather jacket did nothing to hide how muscular, how exquisite his body was. Nor did the dark shaggy hair lessen the impact of his square jaw and hawkish nose and incredible lips.

Good gravy, the guy was gorgeous.

And looking right at you.

He was. It was as if he knew she was looking at the screen at that very second. Piercing gray eyes connected with hers through the video feed, which Billie knew was absolutely ridiculous. He couldn't see her. He had no idea where she was looking, nor even that she'd activated the CCTV camera, but despite that, he was looking at her. Into her soul. Seeing her...

Billie jerked her finger from the control panel and took a step backward, her stare fixed on the now black screen.

Silence wrapped around her, thick and heavy.

Was he still looking at her? Through the inactive camera?

"Billie?"

The almost imperceptible cry of her name made Billie gasp again. Realization hit her, and, face flooding with heat, she rammed her cellphone to her ear.

"Adelaide, what's Gilbert look like?" she asked, studying the control panel of her security system and its black screen. She could *feel* the man outside her gate watching her through the camera. Surely it had to be her mind playing tricks on her? Damn it, her pulse and heart were competing for the title of fastest beating thing in her body.

"Short, five-six at the most," Adelaide answered. "Bit fleshy. Got a paunch. Receding hairline."

"So," Billie said, her heart and pulse increasing in speed, "*not* six-foot plus and completely gorgeous?"

Adelaide barked out a dry laugh. "Not even close."

"Okay, so I'm going to talk to the man at my gate."

"What?" Adelaide yelped.

Jabbing her finger onto the intercom button, Billie leaned closer to the microphone. "Yes?"

"Ms. Sheridan?" the man's deep voice rumbled through the speaker. The kind of voice her acting coach would describe as "panty-creaming".

"Who is this?" Billie asked, utilizing her Destiny voice—the one her character used when facing down malevolent demons and vampires.

"Nathanial Knight, Ms. Sheridan," the man with the panty-creaming voice outside her gate answered. "From Guarded Souls Security and Protection agency."

A little lick of heat traced its way through the pit of Billie's stomach at the way he pronounced her name. Followed by a finger of unease as her brain processed what he'd said.

She pressed the intercom button again. "Did you say Knight?"

A low chortle came as an answer. It was just as deliciously sexy as his voice. Oh God, if it really *was* Gilbert outside trying to fool her, she was going to have a hard time being freaked out by him with a voice and laugh like that.

"Yes, Ms. Sheridan. And yes, I recognize the absurd coincidence of a security expert called Knight coming to the rescue of the star of *Destiny's Knight*."

Billie caught her bottom lip with her teeth, a frown pulling at her eyebrows. The faint sounds of outside wafted through the speaker. Nathanial Knight—if that's who he really was—didn't contribute to any of them.

Pressing her cell phone harder to her ear, she frowned at the black screen. "Adelaide, the man at my gate says he's Nathanial Knight from the security agency."

"Knight?" Adelaide echoed. "Seriously, he said his last name is Knight? Is he kidding?"

"I don't know, but he's—"

Billie stopped herself before she could say *incredibly hot*. What the hell was wrong with her?

Your adrenaline is spiking. Or your libido. One or the other.

The security buzzer sounded again.

"Gotta go," Billie told Adelaide. "It's not Gilbert, so I guess that means the cavalry's arrived."

"Bill—"

Billie killed the connection, and closed the small distance between her and the security control panel.

Mouth dry, muscles tight, she pressed the intercom button again. "Please show me your identification, Mr. Knight."

Without waiting for the man at her gate to answer, she moved her finger to the CCTV button.

The screen filled with a vivid image of him holding his ID up to the camera. Billie didn't miss the crooked smile playing with his lips as he did so. Nor did she miss the way her body responded to that smile.

It had been a while since her body had reacted in such a way. Not since her very private, very brief "relationship" with the show's producer eighteen months ago.

Of course, when said producer told her he was going back to his estranged wife, but that didn't mean they couldn't continue to "see" each other, her bodily reactions to him changed completely.

It made for a charged work environment, which, it seemed, made her energy on the screen electric.

Her heart may have been broken, but her rating had soared.

She'd gone to bed every night since with those high ratings to keep her warm—and a vibrator she affectionately called Roger.

"Give me a moment please," she said, before releasing the intercom button and swiping up a number on her cell.

"Everything okay, Ms. Sheridan?" a mumbling, sleep-slurred voice answered on the other end.

"Hi Riccardo. Sorry for calling in the middle of the night, but can you find something out for me?"

Her personal assistant yawned out a laugh. "Sure."

God love him. He was perfect. So used to dealing with her impulsiveness. She needed to give him a pay rise. "Can you find out if someone called Nathanial Knight works at the Guarded Souls Security and Protection agency, and what he looks like, please?"

"Guarded Souls?" Riccardo grunted. "Cheesy. And seriously? Nathanial Knight?"

"Seriously." She pressed the CCTV button again and narrowed her eyes at the tall streak of hunk waiting calmly for her at her gate. If he was a psycho, he was a patient one.

"Let me just google…" The sound of tapping keys wafted through the phone connection. Did Riccardo have his laptop beside his bed? Just in case his crazy boss asked him for weird information in the middle of the night?

Yeah, she really needed to up his pay.

"Okay," he said, more awake now. "There *is* a security firm called Guarded Souls. The website is very impressive. Looks expensive. Whoa, some of their client testimonials are…wow, Chris Hemsworth is a client? Whoa. Do you think they'd introduce—"

"Riccardo."

He laughed. "Sorry, Ms. Sheridan. Okay, back to the matter at…yeah, yeah, there he is. Nathanial Knight. One of their experts. Dayum, he looks good…um, I mean, he looks intimidating."

She bit her lip, studying Knight through the CCTV screen. *Looks good* didn't even come close. "Describe him, please."

"Do you want the PG or R-rated description?"

"Riccardo."

"Sorry. It's only a head and shoulders shot on the website, but he's got dark hair, what look like gray eyes, a square jaw. Wide shoulders. Looks strong. He clearly works out."

Yep, that was the man at her gate.

"Well, at least I know he's legit," she muttered.

"Legit?" Confusion filled Riccardo's voice. "Are you okay, Ms. Sheridan?"

"I'm okay." Guilt tickled at her. "Sorry for waking you, Riccardo. Thanks for checking that out for me. Go back to sleep."

She ended the call and depressed the intercom button again. "Okay, so you *are* who you say you are."

"I am." Knight smiled, returning his ID to his back pocket, his gaze holding hers through the CCTV camera's lens. "Now I ask, will you invite me in? Please?"

Throat thick, heart racing, stomach an insane mass of butterflies, Billie pressed the button that would unlock the security gate.

It wasn't until she'd opened her front door to find the drop-dead gorgeous man standing on the other side of the threshold that it dawned on her his question had been worded exactly the same way Wraif had first asked permission to enter Destiny's home on the show.

By then, however, it was too late.

She'd opened the door to him.

It was a mistake, of course. It sealed her fate, as well. He'd been watching her for a while, all too aware of her. How could he not be, given what she was?

She didn't know what she'd started by that simple series of actions—the turning of the doorknob, the opening of the door, her gaze finding his—and he could no longer fight that awareness. He'd tried. God knows, he'd tried.

But he was used to failing. It was something he excelled at. The reason for his current situation, as it were. He'd failed to perform to expectation, failed to blindly follow, failed to repress that which he'd felt…and here he was, where Wilhelmina Sheridan *also* was, and no matter what he did, he couldn't deny his awareness of her.

Which brought him to where he was now.

At her door. On her threshold. Looking at her.

He hoped God would forgive him for what he was about to do next, but he knew there was no such luck. God had turned his back on him a long time ago.

Such was the life of a fallen angel.

So, Nathanial Knight, are you ready to fuck up your life a whole lot more?

"Ms. Sheridan," he said, watching her study him. Her heart rate quickened when their eyes connected. He could feel its accelerated beat— an intoxicating rhythm he was already addicted to—moving the very fabric of existence around them both.

Uncertainty, followed by primal lust, and then fear gleamed in her eyes as she studied him. He didn't need to see her hand to know she was gripping the doorknob with white-knuckle pressure.

She had no idea who he was, she questioned whether he was indeed who he *said* he was, but despite that, he affected her.

Just as she did him. The difference was, she'd been affecting him for eons. And he knew how to stop that from showing in his eyes and face.

Billie Sheridan had no such advantage.

Which made standing so close to her now the most difficult thing he'd ever done in the boundless years of his life.

A minute movement in the smooth column of her throat told him she'd swallowed. Was her mouth dry with anticipation? Unease? Or filling with moisture at his proximity? Any option could be the case, and while he could sense so many physical things about her, he did not have the gift of reading her mind or emotions.

An angel born for war was not granted such luxury.

"May I see your identification again, please?" she asked, extending her hand, palm up, toward him.

His body reacted at the husky quality of her voice. His blood ran hotter through his veins.

"You may," he said with a gentle smile, reaching into the back pocket of his jeans to withdraw his wallet once more.

He flipped it open to his ID and offered it to her.

She took it. For a fraction of a second, the tips of her index and middle fingers brushed over his thumb, and it was all he could do to stay motionless as a tsunami of concentrated desire flooded through him.

At Billie's faintest intake of breath, he knew she'd experienced it as well. Her pupils dilated for a heartbeat before she tore her stare from his and directed it at his badge.

Nathanial drew his own breath, keeping it slow and steady.

Curses, he was in trouble. How was he to fight her magnetism now?

He had to, though. If he didn't, who knew what could happen? God alone...and again, God was no longer talking to him.

As Billie studied his ID, he allowed himself a moment to let his gaze roam over the top of her head, her face. Her lashes were long and dark, free of the mascara her job dictated she wear daily.

The long auburn waves of her hair cascaded over her shoulders in a tousled mess, its ends brushing the tops of her breasts.

Nathanial forced himself to draw his gaze away from the curves of flesh concealed by the black cotton of her tank top, lifting his focus back to her face.

Like her lashes, her lips were unadorned by cosmetics, their natural fullness a delicate pink. Why did human females cover their God-given beauty with artificial color? It was a behavior he had never understood, even before being cast out.

"Sorry to keep checking," Billie said, returning her attention to him again, "But there are a lot of weirdos out there."

Direct blue eyes challenged him. Her stare did not waver.

The woman standing before him now exuded control, confidence and not a whisper of fear. And yet, her pulse beat with frenzied speed in her throat.

"I don't mind," he answered, aching to cross her threshold. "And there's no need to be afraid."

Prickly fire erupted in Billie's eyes, a blue inferno of indignance, righteousness and—he couldn't miss it—anger. "Afraid? I'm not afraid, Mr. Knight."

Nathanial bit back his chuckle. "I'm sorry, Ms. Sheridan. I didn't mean to—"

Her cell phone rang, AC/DC's "Highway to

Hell" rocked the room.

She arched a dark red eyebrow at him. "Wait here. Do not move from that spot."

He nodded to show his compliance, even as he frowned.

Still holding his wallet, she walked—backward, her stare fixed on him—to a console table. With the quickest of glances at its surface, she scooped up a smartphone, tapped her thumb over its screen and then lifted the phone to her ear. "Everything okay, Riccardo?"

A brief pause followed as Riccardo answered her.

"Ahh, no it's all good, hon." Her lips curled in a warm smile, the same emotion dancing in her eyes. "Sorry to freak you out. I'm okay. Home. Safe. Can you let Adelaide know I'm okay? I think I may have freaked her out a bit as well earlier."

Nathanial didn't move. He knew of her personal assistant. The young man was efficient and loyal to her. If Nathanial did anything to spook her, with one word from Billie, Riccardo would call the police.

That wouldn't be a good thing.

Still studying him, she let out a low chuckle. "Ask Adelaide. I've got to go." Lowering her phone from her ear, her smile disappeared as she locked her focus on Nathanial once more.

Cautious. She is cautious and intelligent and

not easily fooled.

A finger of admiration traced up Nathanial's spine. She was all those things and so much more. There was a reason he had fallen for—

"If you step across that threshold," she said, "I'll be forced to beat the shit out of you. I'm not quite ready to ask you in yet."

Nathanial blinked at her almost off-handed declaration. "I'm sorry? What?"

Her smile returned, but there was nothing friendly or warm about it. It was the kind of smile he recognized well. The smile of a soldier about to commence battle. "Beat the shit out of you," she repeated. "I can do that. I'm quite adept at it, actually. Put it this way, I've never needed a stunt woman on the show to kick arse."

Arse. The thoroughly non-American pronunciation sent a lick of something tight and hungry through Nathanial. She'd lost her Australian accent within a year of moving to LA. He'd been sad to hear it go, but occasionally the odd inflection from her formative years slipped out, sounding at odds with the exotically ambiguous accent she had now.

Letting his own lips stretch once again into an affable smile, he inclined his head in a single nod. "I don't doubt it."

She ran a quick look over him. He barely

resisted the urge to shuffle on his feet at the inspection. What would she think if she really knew who—*what*—she was looking at?

"Good. Now, tell me why you're here."

With a relaxed, unhurried move, Nathanial rested his elbow against the doorjamb next to his head. "To get my *arse* kicked by you?"

He'd spent almost fifty years in Australia a century ago. He could speak Strayan, as the locals called it, with the best of them if needed.

Billie arched an eyebrow at him. "How's a broken clavicle sound?"

"Painful," he answered honestly. The last being to break his clavicle was his fellow angel, Erah, three millennia ago.

She crossed her arms over her breasts with an expectant expression.

It dawned on him she wore only a loose pair of black boxer shorts to go with her black tank top. Her feminine form called to him, fit and toned and subtly muscled.

He knew she worked out. He also knew she'd failed to pass her black-belt ranking when she was a teenager in Sydney. She still trained in the martial arts, despite never trying to achieve the venerated belt again, and her technique and speed were impressive. He'd also witnessed the strength of her body at work both on set and in the gym. And she jogged. She loved to jog. Her fitness levels were admirable.

Before he could stop himself, he took in the perfection of her exposed legs. Every part of his body tightened. Various parts of his body grew thicker. Harder.

"Oi, pretty boy."

He startled at her blunt exclamation. *Startled.* When was the last time he'd startled? Not since he'd been cast out, that was for certain. Definitely not since his time began among mortals here on Earth.

Jerking his gaze up to her face, he found her studying him with a mocking frown. "You really *do* want to get your arse kicked, don't you?"

Scratching at the hair on the back of his head, he gave her an apologetic grimace. "I apologize, Ms. Sheridan. I'm not used to being in the company of a bona fide celebrity. Especially one wearing so few clothes. My boss warned me you would break my—"

Her phone rang again.

"Don't move," she instructed, connecting the call. "What's up, Riccardo?"

Riccardo said something. For a moment, Nathanial considered allowing himself to hear what the personal assistant was saying but thought better of it. Being here already was dangerous. Drawing attention to where he was…it wasn't a smart move. And using the *abilities* still afforded to him after being cast out would *more* than draw attention to his location. There were other forces moving about in the world of man, malevolent forces of unending power and bottomless hate that would cherish the opportunity to destroy one of God's soldiers, even a fallen one.

"No no, hon," Billie said, watching Nathanial from her position beside the console table. "Honestly, I'm fine. No, I don't need you here. I'm good. Promise."

Whatever Riccardo said made her laugh.

Nathanial bit back a groan at the exquisite sound. An angel was not meant to be drawn to sinful sensations, and yet everything about Billie Sheridan's laugh suggested that very thing: sin of the pleasurable variety.

He was screwed. In every metaphorical sense there was.

"As if I'm going to do that," she said to Riccardo, something close to devilment playing with her lips. "Now bugger off with you."

She ended the call with a jab of her thumb.

He waited on the other side of the threshold. If his wings had been present, they would have been fanned wide and poised.

Thank God Billie couldn't see them.

Thank God? Huh. When is that ever going to get old?

"Okay," she said, giving her head a little jerk. "You can come in."

Nathanial steeled himself against the impact on every molecule in his body caused by the simple, innocent invitation.

That impact came: a rush of desire, of need, of power, of hunger. The one living soul he'd been waiting on for over three hundred years, the reason he'd been cast out of Heaven.

Billie Sheridan had invited him into her home.

He stepped across the threshold.

Instantly, her scent filled his being. He didn't just breathe her in—angels, even fallen ones, had no real need for breath, drawing it was an assumed affectation to avoid detection amongst man. He filled himself with her presence. The delicate perfume of her natural scent, the lingering kiss of the soap she'd used to bathe, the fruity sweetness of her shampoo, her femininity…

A rush of hot longing smashed through him at the unexpected but unmistakable scent of her arousal.

She was turned on by him.

His nostrils flared and he brought himself to a halt a few steps into her home. He feared what he'd do if he stepped closer to her.

She watched him. He didn't miss the quick swipe of her tongue over her lips.

What would she do if he destroyed the distance between them, hauled her to his body and crushed her lips with his?

Would she kiss him back? Would she surrender to that which her body wanted? Or would she, to use her own words, beat the shit out of him?

"So, Mr. Knight." She scratched at the side of her nose in a relaxed action he recognized as belonging to her television character. "Do you know about this stalker of mine?"

"I do."

"Tell me about him. Is his name really Gilbert? Gilbert what?"

Nathanial turned his head, letting his gaze roam over her living room and its dark windows. "Gilbert Sanders."

"And what does Gilbert Sanders do when he's not stalking me?"

Her blasé attitude was an act. He didn't need to be one of God's soldiers to see that. She was an incredible actress, but right at that point, she was stiffer than a board. Trying to hide it, of course, but stiff. On edge.

He didn't blame her.

"Gilbert," he said, making his way into her living room even, as he kept as much distance from her as possible without looking like he was, "is a high school geography teacher."

She burst out laughing.

It took him completely by surprise. His feet faltered beneath him and he would have tripped if not for his wings. Not present in this realm, but still connected to him, they were invisible to everyone. Except Nathanial. He'd been amongst man for centuries now, and whenever he glimpsed his wings in the reflection of a mirror or window or shiny surface, he still experienced a split second of panic his true form had been exposed.

His wings—not so white as they once were—were still something to behold.

"A geography teacher?"

Billie's laughter danced in her question. Nathanial knew it was wrong to be happy for that laughter, given her situation, and yet he couldn't help but smile.

Lowering himself into a simple white-leather armchair he suspected cost an obscene amount of money, he rested his ankle on his bent knee and watched her join him in the living room.

He appreciated the natural grace with which she lowered herself into the armchair opposite him—this one round and vivid orange with a lime-green pillow featuring a portrait of Yoda from *Star Wars*.

"Tell me about him," she instructed, curling her legs beneath her. Should he suggest she put on more clothes?

It was the decent thing to do.

But he *was* a fallen angel. Didn't that allow

him to forget decent?

Doing everything he could to keep his gaze on hers, he uncrossed his leg, leaned forward in the armchair and rested his elbows on his knees. "Gilbert Sanders believes you and him are meant to be together forever, and he's proven he will stop at nothing to make that happ—"

A sharp buzzing filled the room, cutting Nathanial short.

Uncertainty and confusion flickered over Billie's face. A frown pulled at her straight eyebrows. She stared at him hard for a second before flicking the front door to her home a quick look. No, not the front door, the security control panel next to it.

Nathanial bit back a curse, fighting to keep his expression calm. He hadn't planned on them being interrupted so quickly. What the hell was Kade doing? The vampire was supposed to keep the authorities from—

"I'm just going to see who's at the gate," he said, straightening from the armchair.

"No no." Billie unfurled from her seat. Tension radiated from her. "I'll get it. It's probably the LAPD and they'll want to hear from me first. Don't want them getting antsy, do we."

Nathanial ground his teeth as she began walking toward the control panel. How did he take charge of this without making her suspicious?

"Goddamn it," he muttered, throwing the ceiling a harried look.

Was the blasphemous exclamation noted? Did it even matter anymore?

"Billie," he called, striding toward her.

Damn it. Damn it. Damn it.

She didn't slow down. "Ms. Sheridan," she corrected without looking at him.

Two paces. She was a mere two paces from the control panel. Two paces from discovering the police—

"Screw it," he said under his breath, as he traversed the distant between them in a heartbeat.

It was a heartbeat too long.

As he reformed directly behind her, the moment every molecule in his body knitted together with agonizing power and speed, Billie pressed her finger to the control panel's intercom button. "Who's this?"

"Ms. Sheridan?" a gravelly male voice sounded through the panel's speaker. "This is Detective Rhames from LAPD. I'm sorry for disturbing you at such an hour, but there's something I need to talk to you about. Your agent, Adelaide Williams, informed you I was coming, yes?"

"Yes. Along with someone from a security

agency."

"Yeah, Gary Rosetti from Guard-U Protection. He's about five minutes away, I think."

"Fuck," Nathanial sighed, balling his fists. His wings flexed.

Billie startled and spun around, her stare locking on his, realization dawning in her eyes.

And then, without warning, she slammed her fist into his jaw.

He rolled his head with the punch, the shock of her knuckles crunching against his skin and bone dulled by his admiration for her ferocity.

When she tried to follow up that punch with another, however, he acted.

Fast.

Faster than she could see.

Faster than any human could track.

Without a word, he wrapped his fingers around her wrist before her second punch could land, spun her around until her back was mashed against his chest, his other hand covering her mouth, and whispered in her ear, "Time to get the hell out of here, Ms. Sheridan."

Chapter Two

Shock froze Billie.

Her blood roared in her ears, her head spun. She stood stock-still in Knight's imprisoning arms, her heart the only thing moving.

It smashed up into her throat, wild and fast and frenzied.

What the hell was going on? What the hell—

She jerked up her knee and drove her heel into the top of his foot.

Her heel encountered what felt like solid granite.

Instant pain exploded in her foot, up her leg, into her hip. She cried out against his palm, hot tears stinging her eyes. It was only the fact that Knight grunted at the contact that told her she hadn't heeled the floor. What the hell were the guy's shoes made from?

"Billie," he groaned in her ear, his arms drawing her harder to his chest. There was no pain in his voice, only exasperation, and—of all things—an apology. "I will explain everything later, I promise. But I swear, I'm not here to hurt you."

"Yeah, right," she mumbled against his palm.

"If I remove my hand from your mouth, you have to promise me not to scream, okay?"

A dry laugh tore at Billie's chest. Sure. As if she was going to promise him anything.

She dragged in a breath through her nostrils—and whimpered as the most delicious, intoxicating smell she'd ever experienced flowed into her nose. Her whole body reacted. Her. Whole. Body. Her pulse leaped into crazy flight, her stomach fluttered and flip-flopped, and her sex…whoa.

Who the hell *was* this guy?

The buzzer of her security intercom split the silence.

Billie flinched. Knight muttered something in a language she didn't understand.

Yeah, be worried, jerk, she thought.

"Promise me, Billie," he repeated, his lips grazing her temple.

A sudden and compelling urge to turn her head, to lift her face until those lips of his grazed her own flooded through her. She could already feel his tongue touching hers, could feel his palm as it cupped her breast. Could feel the thick, long pole of his erection as it ground to her—

Icy confusion and shock lashed at her. What the fuck was she thinking? What the fuck was she *doing*?

She thrashed in his arms, wild and crazy. She knew all the techniques for escaping a hold such as this one, but at that very second, all the techniques meant diddly-squat. A hot-as-hell stranger who smelled like heaven and filled her with an aching hunger for sinful sex was holding her captive. Rational thought and years of training were no match for that kind of assault.

"Billie," Knight growled, refusing to release her. The bastard. And she was flailing and thrashing so hard as well. "Stop it."

Her security buzzer sounded again, the perfect soundtrack to the scene.

She bucked in his arms. God, if her stunt director could see her now...

"Enough," the towering, sexy-as-sin and equally scary man snarled, hauling her completely off her feet. "We don't have time for this. He's coming. And he's stronger than I—"

Billie jack-knifed her legs upward with such abrupt force, Knight staggered backward. A splintering creek told her he'd slammed into the console table a fraction of a second before his arms loosened around her.

It was all she needed.

Turning her body to a limp noodle, she slipped downward. Out of his grasp.

Her knees connected with the floor with a clunk. Pain erupted, sharp and cold.

She didn't take the time to acknowledge it. Launching herself to her feet, she struck her right heel into Knight's gut in a brutal back-kick her old tae kwon do instructor would have been proud of, driving Knight backward into the console table again.

The sound of breaking glass filled the room as her People's Choice Award tumbled off the table and shattered on the floor.

Billie didn't wait for Knight's reaction. Channeling all her repressed anger at failing her black belt grading all those years ago, she threw herself into a jumping spinning kick, her heel crunching against his cheekbone with beautiful force and precision.

He went down.

Hard.

For a moment, just a moment, as Billie landed on the balls of her feet, her pulse and heart crazy, her stare locked on him, she could have sworn the air behind his back shimmered with white pearlescent energy.

"What the..." she whispered, as what

looked like two massive wings of white feathers seemed to form.

He groaned, planting a palm on the floor beside his shoulder.

Her security buzzer sounded again.

Billie blinked, and the space at his back was just that—space.

She turned and fled, running for the front door.

"Billie!"

She didn't stop, falter or turn at his shout. Instead, she smacked her palm against the control panel, unlocking the security gate as she yanked open the door.

The hot summer night wrapped around her with greedy passion as she ran from her home. Her bare feet slapped on the slate entry stairs. Her hair whipped around her shoulders.

"Ms. Sheridan?" a male voice—high with startled confusion—called from the blackness of her front yard before her. "Ms. Sheridan, is everything—"

A vise captured her wrist, jerking her off her feet.

She squealed. An honest-to-goodness squeal. When was the last time she'd squealed?

Knight covered her mouth with a hard palm, smothering the sound.

She bit him. Sank her teeth into his flesh as hard as she could.

"Hey!" he exclaimed, his other arm clamping around her waist. He didn't remove his hand from her mouth.

"Ms. Sheridan?" the other male voice called, growing closer. Detective Rhames? Was her savior about to save her from her savior?

"I'm sorry, Billie," Knight rasped against her temple. "I didn't want you to see this."

She bucked and kicked. And then grew motionless as a man roughly the size of an office block wearing an ill-fitting blue suit ran out of the shadows of the night directly in front of them on the path.

He skidded to a halt when his stare fell on them. With impressive speed, his service pistol was in his hand, pointed at Knight's head. "Let her go," he demanded, the authority in his voice absolute.

Detective Rhames was an intimidating individual.

"Can't do that, Rhames," Knight replied, clearly intimidated to a point of deluded stupidity.

Confusion flickered in Rhames's steely stare. There and gone just as quick. Replaced by steely resolve. "I don't know who you are, bud, but you need to release Ms. Sheridan now before I—"

"I'm Nathanial Knight," Knight said with relaxed calm, his grip on her body not even remotely slackening. "And you're going to lower your gun."

The faintest of frowns played with Rhames's eyebrows—and then he let out a soft laugh. "Of course I am." He tucked his gun back into its holster and gave it a happy pat. "See?"

Billie blinked. She would have gaped if Knight's hand wasn't still covering her mouth.

Behind her, Knight nodded, his chin tapping the top of her head a few times. "Excellent. Now tell me, Rhames, who else is here? Is your partner with you? A squad car on the way?"

A loose smile stretched Rhames's lips. "No, sir, it's just me right now, but a squad car *is* on the way. And Gary from Guard-U won't be that far behind."

Once again, Knight muttered something in that peculiar language Billie couldn't understand. A shiver rippled up her spine. Her nipples pebbled.

She growled in exasperated frustration against Knight's palm. What the hell was she doing getting turned on by some words she didn't know, uttered by a guy who was equally unfamiliar? Surely the fact he was doing some freaky Jedi mind thing to Detective Rhames was enough to destroy any misguided attraction she'd felt for him when he first entered her home? That, and the fact he seemed hell bent on abducting her.

Her scalp prickled at the surreal thought and, ridiculously, a silent, shaky chuckle bubbled up in her chest. Being turned on and scared at the same time; she'd need to draw on this moment the next time she was filming a scene with Wraif. The real Wraif. Well, the actor who played the real Wraif. Not the stalker Gilbert who thought he was the real Wraif.

Oh God, she was going to start freaking out soon if she didn't get away.

Then get away. Now.

The second the thought drilled through her head, she began to fight Knight's hold.

She thrashed about, screaming against his palm, bucking and kicking, staring at Rhames the whole time.

The detective watched her with a relaxed smile. He didn't react to the sight of her struggling to be free. Knight continued to hold her, having no difficulty doing so, she was dismayed to note.

"Can you do me a favor, Rhames?" he asked, raising his voice a little when she increased her protests behind his palm.

"Absolutely," Rhames replied with puppy-dog exuberance. "Name it."

"Can you radio in that Ms. Sheridan is fine, safe, and you've set up a detail on her, please?"

A giddy wave washed over Billie at the

unspoken implication in Knight's request. Her knees wobbled.

Oh no. Oh no oh no oh no.

With another wide smile, Rhames nodded. "I can do that."

"Good work," Knight said. "Any chance you can also contact Gary and tell him his services are no longer required?"

Rhames nodded again. "Definitely." He pivoted on his heel and began to walk back down the dark path toward Billie's gate and the street beyond.

"No!" Billie cried into Knight's hand, resuming her desperate thrashing.

"Rhames?" Knight called over her shoulder, his arms like velvet-steel bands around her body.

The detective stopped and turned back, eying Knight with an enthusiasm that turned her already sinking stomach. "Yes, Nathanial Knight?"

"Make sure Billie isn't disturbed by anyone."

"Absolutely, sir," Rhames agreed.

"And Rhames?" Knight called again, drawing Billie closer. Close enough for her to become aware of him on a level she didn't want to acknowledge or accept. God, he not only smelled like heaven, he felt like it as—

"You never saw me, and you have no idea who Nathanial Knight is, got it?"

Rhames grinned and tapped his fingers to the peak of an invisible cap. "Got it."

And with that, he turned and hurried into the darkness, whistling as he went.

Whistling "Ode to Joy," of all things.

The jubilant, stress-free sound was too much for Billie. She slumped in Knight's arms, defeated. Something had just happened that made no freaking sense. Something weird and unnatural and she couldn't process it. Not while she was directing energy into trying to escape a hold that was clearly inescapable.

She needed to regroup.

She needed distance from him. She'd brought him down with a back-kick and a spinning kick earlier. She could do it again, as long as he wasn't holding her. As long as she wasn't feeling his hard, sculpted body rubbing against hers. As long as she wasn't breathing in his intoxicating scent.

Oh boy.

"Okay," Knight murmured against her temple. "I'm going to let go of you. Don't do anything we'll both regret."

"Okay," she mumbled against his palm.

He chuckled. He actually chuckled.

God help her, she liked the sound of it.

For a moment, neither of them moved. Knight held her close, his chest to her back, his groin near her butt. She tried not to think about how aware she was of *that* fact, but despite the surreal situation—the apparently hypnotized Detective Rhames, Gilbert the Stalker, the...the...wings?—she couldn't help but notice how hard and large and bulgy his groin was.

Her head swam. Her nipples beaded. An inexplicable hunger washed over her, making her skin prickle and the junction of her thighs grow warm.

A choked whimper tore at her throat. What was going on?

"Please don't do anything we'll regret," Knight whispered against her temple, his arms loosening around her.

What? Like kiss you?

The ridiculous thought tickled her sanity as he released her.

She stepped clear of him. Three steps. Three hurried steps. And then turned around and studied him.

Out here, in the dark, with only the glow from the fat summer moon and the muted ankle-high lights of her garden to illuminate him, she could barely discern his features. And yet, he seemed to somehow draw her eye, as if he was the only thing in existence worth her attention. Which was a load of hooey, because the Emmys were just around the corner.

"Who are you?" she asked, surprised at how

husky her voice was. She pinched her thumbnail with her fingertips. "*What* are you?"

He arched an eyebrow, the feel the action stirring something in her soul. It made no sense, but it did. She could *feel* it on a visceral, tangible level. "'What'?"

"I said," she repeated, fixing her stare hard on his dark shape, "who are you. *What* are you?"

A relaxed laugh fell from him. Billie's nipples pinched at the wicked sound. "Oh no, I heard you. I was just clarifying you'd used the word *what*."

She rolled her eyes and shook her head. "I can tell you what you're *not*," she said.

"What's that?"

"A comedian."

He laughed. The relaxed sound rose up into the night. A shiver of traitorous delight wicked up her spine.

"Or normal," she finished, teeth gritted. She had to get a control of all her weird sexual reactions to him. She was pretty damn certain he was on the verge of attempting to abduct her; getting turned on by him wasn't the appropriate reaction to such a situation.

"Normal?" he repeated, taking one step toward her. The moon's glow found him and for a moment, Billie forgot entirely how to breathe.

"W...w..." It was the only sound she could

make. Her brain, her mouth, her tongue and her lips had no hope of working together to form the word *wings*.

Wings. He had wings. Beautiful, majestic, massive, feathered wings.

He had *wings*.

"Define normal."

She blinked at his instruction. And the wings were gone. Whatever messed-up trick of the light had made her see them was finished. No more wings, just a man sexier than any guy had a right to be, slowly stalking her with unequivocal intent and a smolder in his eye that would put Ryan Gosling to shame.

Hey girl, you should be running right now...

She stumbled back a step.

Knight continued to move toward her. "The word *normal* is incredibly subjective." His voice caressed her sanity, and her breath grew shallow. "What's normal for me may not, in any way, shape or form, be normal for Detective Rhames."

Billie swallowed. How was he so close to her again? Why wasn't she kicking his arse? Why wasn't she screaming? Or running away?

Why aren't you kissing him? Why aren't you tearing his clothes off and mounting him like a—

"What did you do to Rhames?" she croaked, stumbling back another step. Her heart hammered in her throat. Her stare locked on his face. God, he was gorgeous. And scary. "Are you a hypnotist?"

"If I am?" he countered, drawing closer still. So close that intoxicating scent tickled her senses once more. Her body reacted. The urge, no, the *need* to close the distance between them, tangle her fingers in his hair and kiss him damn near overwhelmed her.

"Vegas is four-hundred twenty kilometers east," she answered, watching him. "I mean, three-hundred miles. Ish."

He laughed. Threw back his head and laughed.

The trees and plants in her garden seemed to laugh with him, rustling and swaying in a breeze Billie didn't feel on her face. The moonlight played with him again. And once again, the air behind him seemed to be…different.

"When I count to three and click my fingers, Billie Sheridan," he said, but a mere step away from her now (when the hell had she stopped backing away?), "you will be under my power. One." He closed the small space between them. "Two." She gazed up at him, into his eyes. Eyes the color of a stormy Sunday. "Three."

He raised his hand and clicked his fingers in the space beside their heads.

Billie gasped.

He lowered his head closer to hers, eyebrow cocked.

"Fuck you," she rasped.

He chuckled again. And again, her body reacted. On a carnal level she'd never experienced before.

She drew a deep breath and retreated a step. If this was Stockholm Syndrome, surely her mind should wait until Knight had actually abducted her. And kept her captive for a few days. Right?

Her mouth dry, her lips the same, she narrowed her eyes and studied him. If he was a psychopath, he was the most gorgeous one on the planet. But then again, hadn't this country's most famous serial killer, Ted Bundy, been attractive?

"Please tell me what's going on? Without any bullshit and charm, okay?" she asked. The fact she wasn't running, wasn't screaming, should worry her. But as surreal and weird as this whole thing was, something deep inside her, something her religious aunt would have called her soul, felt...safe. (If her very religious aunt was still talking to her, that was, and not denying her existence due to her "blasphemous and abhorrent" role as Destiny on an equally "abhorrent and blasphemous" show.) "What the hell is going on? Who are you and what do you want with me?"

Knight remained motionless. His gaze held hers, unwavering and direct.

She didn't blink. Didn't look away. Her heart raced in her throat as she narrowed her eyes and tilted her chin.

"Gilbert Sanders," Knight said, his voice calm, his expression unreadable, "has sold his soul to Satan to make you his, and there is only one being who can stop that from happening— me."

Okay, he hadn't meant to lay it on the line quite so bluntly. But then, he also hadn't planned to influence an LAPD detective, either. Roanon Rhames was a good man, with a strong heart, stronger soul and a family he loved more than anything. Nathanial had sought out that strong soul of his the moment the man stood before them and, in the time it took his heart to beat once, watched Rhames's entire life play out. Experienced it on every level an angel could in the blink of an eye. Rhames was one of the good ones, and as such, Nathanial didn't like *influencing* his free will to do what Nathanial wanted him to do.

But if he hadn't, both Rhames *and* Billie would be in danger. Thanks to an unknown being of powerful force, Gilbert Sanders was more dangerous than a simple geography teacher had a right to be, with a single-minded goal. Rhames would not fare well if he were to come face to face with Gilbert.

The obsessed fan was now a threat beyond the comprehension of man. Nathanial couldn't risk Billie's safety—or the detective's—by playing it safe.

Forcing his body and mind to stay calm, almost detached, he held Billie's stare.

She frowned, digesting what he'd said. "Sold his soul to…Satan?" A nervous giggle fell from her lips. "Are you for real?" Her frown deepened, even as a puzzled smile tugged at the corners of her lips. "You're kidding, right?" She suddenly straightened and, scratching at the side of her nose, swung her gaze around the dark garden surrounding them. "Am I being pranked?"

Nathanial bit back a curse. "Billie, I'm afraid I'm not kidding. I know this sounds absurd, but you must believe me. For your safety and the safety of those around you, we need to leave here, now."

"So Gilbert the soulless stalker can't make me his?"

He didn't miss the mocking disbelief in her question. He couldn't blame her. If *he* were a man, rather than an angel expelled from Heaven for the audacity to feel something more for a human than his creation dictated, he wouldn't believe a word he was saying, either.

That didn't change anything though. He had to get her out of here.

He could do it one of three ways. He could influence her, in the same way he'd compelled Rhames to do his bidding; he could quite simply ignore any of her protests and straight-up physically take her away (not exactly his top choice, given his jaw was still tingling from her earlier right hook and his solar plexus was still throbbing from her earlier kick); or he could convince her with charm and logic.

Charm and logic were what he was gambling on. Of course, he'd never had any real success with those techniques when he *wasn't* fallen, so why he had any chance now...

Hope. Hope and dread. That was what he had. Hope she would come without causing a fuss, and dread they wouldn't get away before Gilbert arrived.

And determination.

He had been cast aside because of Wilhelmina Sheridan.

His very existence was altered irrevocably because of her.

He would not now, or ever, allow Gilbert to have her.

He would get her to safety, deal with the obsessed fan, and then he would locate the unknown being who had given the geography teacher such unnatural power and deal with them as well.

He'd been a Second Sphere Power before his expulsion, one of God's fiercest warriors. The unknown being *would* suffer.

"Billie," he repeated, holding back the power to render her free will void with strained control, "I promise I will not hurt you. But we must leave now."

She studied him, expression enigmatic. "As long as you *promise*," she said. Sarcasm dripped from the word. "Let me get my coat."

She moved. Faster than he'd expected.

Without warning, she launched into a sprint, running past him. Headed along the shadowy path toward her front gate.

"Ah, sod it," Nathanial muttered, pivoting on his heel to follow her.

He should have known this wasn't going to go smoothly. He'd watched her for her whole life. She wasn't a doormat or a chump by any means. Gullible was never a word he'd use to describe her.

Fighter. Feisty. Playful. Creative. Loopy. Loyal. Generous. *They* were the words he'd use. Along with kind, giving, stubborn and sarcastic.

He'd fallen in love with her for all those words.

Of course, now some of those words— stubborn, came to mind—were going to make this situation go pear-shape if he didn't…

"Sod it," he repeated, fixing his stare on her back. "Billie," he called, releasing a tiny ribbon of his will. Not a lot; just enough to snag hers.

She faltered to a halt and turned to look at him. Her eyes were wide. Her lips were parted. Her breasts heaved. The wild mess of burnt-copper waves tumbled around her face and shoulders in a cascade of silken strands he longed to feel trickling through his fingers.

God save him, she was beautiful.

He crossed to where she stood with slowed strides.

She didn't move. His will tangled in hers, an intangible knot she had no hope of escaping.

"Billie," he said again, a low, calm affirmation that it was okay, everything was okay…

"Knight?" she responded, not moving.

Her will strained against the bind he'd placed upon it. Rebelled. But it was all for naught. Like Detective Rhames, she was under his influence.

Fuck.

She gazed up at him, her eyes almost ice blue in the moon's silver glow, her skin smooth and flawless in its natural beauty.

You need to walk into your home, pack an overnight bag, and then leave with me. Now.

The instruction formed in his mind, concise

and perfect.

He stepped closer. Closer. So close, the delicate scent of everything she was caressed him. A scent, an existence, a reality he'd known for over three hundred years.

"You need to kiss me," he said, the instruction little more than a scratchy breath.

A smile of sheer joy stretched Billie's lips and, with a soft sigh of acquiescence, she closed the distance between them, combed her fingers through the hair at his nape and drew his head down to hers.

Her parted lips brushed Nathanial's, gentle and tender at first, like a tentative invitation.

An electrical charge jolted through him. His heart—an organ of divine creation and significance—thumped hard and fast.

A gasp tore from him. A groan. His entire body erupted in an inferno of hungry need and aching desire. His head swam. His wings flexed and spread. His groin...his groin throbbed with a molten urgency.

Nathanial froze.

He hadn't been prepared for this. It was more intense, more profound, than he'd ever imagined.

He'd never hoped Billie Sheridan's lips would ever touch his, but now...

Billie parted her lips more, seeking out his tongue with hers. Finding it. Sliding against it.

She pressed her body to his, her breasts crushing against his chest.

Another groan rumbled deep in his chest, and he smoothed his hands over his hips, drawing her closer.

She was kissing him, something he'd ached for since he'd stolen a look into the endless expanse of the future three hundred years ago and saw her. She was kissing him.

But she wasn't. Not really.

A cold finger of guilt drilled into Nathanial's chest.

He'd taken control of her free will. Her lips may be on his, her tongue may be seeking his out, the exquisite perfection of her body—with all its soft curves and dips and planes—may be pressed to his, her fingers may be tangled in his hair and the divine curve of her sex may be nestled against the growing bulge of his groin, but Billie Sheridan wasn't kissing him.

He pulled away from her with a tormented growl and, gut a broiling mess of self-disgust, released his will's influence over hers.

She stumbled back a step. Stared at him. Raised a shaking hand to her mouth.

He watched her trace her fingertips over her lips, lips still moist from their kiss.

"H-how did you…" She stopped. Caught her bottom lip with her teeth, confusion warring with horror in her eyes as she looked at him. "How did you make me…"

She didn't finish. Whether because she couldn't bring herself to vocalize the mental *and* physical assault he'd just subjected her to, or because she still couldn't comprehend what had just happened, he didn't know.

Tortured uncertainty radiated from her.

The emotion ripped him apart. Made him hate himself. Angels, even fallen ones, rarely experienced hate. It served no purpose. And yet, Nathanial felt it now.

Hate. Thick and sour and dark.

Lord save him, what had he done? What had he been thinking?

And how did he move forward, knowing how heinous he'd behaved?

"How did you do that?" she finally asked, the words a scratchy, tormented breath.

Drawing in a slow breath of his own, Nathanial stepped closer to her again, close enough that the shadows of the night would not be able to hide his face from her. He lowered his head until she could see the whites of his eyes and said, "An angel has the power to render the free will of a human null and void when required."

Something dark and icy glinted in Billie's eyes. Her jaw bunched. Her heart beat hard enough he could not only hear it, but feel it disturb the air around them. "*Null and void?*

That's what you call what you just did?"

The anger in her voice raked against Nathanial's guilt like a razor-tipped hook.

"I can influence the actions of man, Wilhelmina Sheridan," he said with matter-of-fact calm, "but I cannot influence what they are genuinely feeling deep in their very soul. And by the way you kissed me just then…"

Her eyes narrowed. "For an angel," she said lowly, "you're a complete prick."

"Ask your soul if you truly believe that to be true," he shot back.

What the fuck was wrong with him? Was he truly standing in her front yard, arguing with her about the kiss he'd compelled her to give him? Was he losing his sanity, standing this close to her? Was God punishing him more for what he'd done by causing his rational mind to erode in her presence?

He didn't see her punch. He sensed the displaced air a fraction of a second before her fist smashed into his jaw. The second time she'd landed such a blow on his person since he'd made himself known to her.

He staggered sideways under the force, not so much unbalanced, but unsettled. How must she loathe him, fear him, to strike out at him so.

"Get away from me or I'll break your fucking jaw," she snarled.

It was nothing less than what he deserved, but the fact offered Nathanial no peace. Self-disgust and self-contempt roped through him. She would never trust him now. Not after this. His lack of discipline, his failure to control himself, had put Billie in more danger than if he'd never come near her.

"Billie…" He held up his hands, palms out, pouring every ounce of his desperation and conviction into his voice. "I *can't* get away from you. I can't leave you. I have to protect you, or you'll experience something far more heinous than me *influencing* you. If I were to leave you to Gilbert's lust, it won't just be your body, but your mind and soul subjected to his depraved sexual appetites and insane obsession."

"Says you," she shot back.

But she didn't run. Nor did she shrink away from him.

It wasn't much, but it was something.

At this point, Nathanial would take *something*, no matter how small.

Let her see you, really see you. Then she will truly understand.

"Billie…" He took a slow step toward her. He kept his palms facing her, his gaze on her face. "I apologize for what I did. I shouldn't have allowed my…my feelings for you to jeopardize your safety. But we must go. Together. Now."

Her eyes narrowed. "*Feelings* for me? Given we've only known each other for approximately twenty seconds, I can't fathom you having any kind of feelings for me I'd want to know about."

Nathanial drew in a slow breath. "I can erase the moment from your memory if you wish, or I can compel your will to do as I wish again. I don't want to do either. You can believe I'm insane, but the one thing I do *not* want you to believe is that I don't know you. I've known you for every second of your life."

Billie's eyebrows shot up. "Oh, well, that's completely reassuring."

Warmth radiated through Nathanial. She was so feisty. So sarcastic.

"Remind me again why I should be running away from Gilbert and not you?"

"Because—" He stopped at the finger of ice tracing up his spine. At the sudden metallic taint to the very air. At the whisper of insanity on the breeze.

Straightening, he scanned the darkness and shadows around them.

Gilbert. Gilbert was here. Now. He'd arrived. And the emptiness of his freely given soul was far more imbued with the Dark One's force than Nathanial had expected.

Every muscle in Nathanial's body coiled. His gut clenched.

They'd run out of time. Billie had run out of time.

"Because," he said, returning his focus to Billie, "unlike Gilbert, I have these."

And with a shudder, he released the shield concealing his wings from the sight of man, and flexed them out to their fullest span.

Billie's eyes widened. She stumbled back a step.

"Holy fuck," she breathed.

"If only," Nathanial murmured, before snaking his arm around her waist, hauling her to his body and launching them both into the night sky with one powerful downward thrust of his wings.

Chapter Three

What. The holy. Fuck?

She clung to the hard, warm body of the…the…*angel* as the hot night air whipped through her hair and at her face.

Angel.

An angel had grabbed her—*abducted* her—and was now flying through the night sky, taking her…somewhere.

Her head swam.

No, no. You can't pass out. You can't.

She clung tighter to Knight. It was that or plummet to her death.

"God help me," she muttered against his chest, eyes squeezed shut.

"As if," the angel rumbled, the words like thunder against her lips.

God loves us. All of us.

Her mother's words whispered through her head, almost feverish in their intensity, which was always the way her mother spoke of God— feverishly, zealously and ardently.

Huh. Her mother had probably never expected her only daughter to one day be wrapped around a freaking angel and flying who knows how high above LA at 2 am in the morning.

Still, her mother *had* promised her God loved everyone, and now here was this git with wings—albeit a sexy git with wings—telling her otherwise?

Yeah, no ball, dude.

Squeezing her arms tighter around Knight's torso, and adding her legs around his hips for good measure, she pulled her head from his chest and glared at him. A distant part of her mind excitedly informed her that he truly did seem very well endowed below the waist, but that part of her mind could just shut the hell up. "I know I'm in no position to say this, but screw you."

The stupid wind whipped the words away. Great. How fast were they flying? Where were they flying *to*?

His angry-ocean gray eyes fixed on hers and his lips curled. Goddamn it, he had a gorgeous smile. "I'm not that kind of angel." His gaze dipped to her mouth for a fleeting second.

"Although, I must admit, I *have* wondered about the logistics of mid-flight copulation."

The junction of her thighs grew warm. That distant part of her mind immediately flung up an image of them hurtling through space in a position usually only found in bed. Damn it.

She narrowed her glare. "You'd have to Jedi mind-trick me. *Again.*"

Something dark and ominous flared in his eyes, and her breath caught in her throat. "Please don't Jedi mind-trick me," she squeaked.

What the hell was she doing, antagonizing him like that? It was a long way down to the ground.

He slid his stare away from her face, fixing it instead on the direction they were headed.

Up? It could be. Or it could be sideways. She couldn't tell. Her hair lashed about her head in every direction, and the pull on her stomach...well, it wasn't like the kind of sensation she equated with going up or down fast on a roller coaster or in an elevator. Her brain told her they were moving, fast, but her body had no idea which way.

Maybe you're not flying? Maybe he's messing with your head and you're standing outside your home?

"You're not."

She gasped at his low statement, and glared

at him harder. "Listen, none of this is fun. But if you're reading my mind, you can just get the hell out of there. No trespassing. Got it?"

"Got it. And I didn't mean to. I just…" His jaw bunched and his arm around her waist grew tighter. "It's a strong mind you've got there, Wilhelmina Sheridan. Powerful. Potent. It's hard to deny it."

Her heart leapt faster at the surreal declaration. "Deny…" She frowned and shook her head, even as she adjusted her legs around his hips. "I'm dreaming. Have to be."

His deep chest vibrated against her breasts as he chuckled. "Will it help you to believe that? I can make—"

"Don't even try it, dude."

His teeth flashed in a smile no angel had any right smiling. Wicked and full of promise.

The junction of her thighs grew warmer. Her pulse quickened. Grinding her teeth, she squeezed her eyes shut and pressed her forehead to his impressive pec. "If you don't mind, I'm just going to smoosh my face against your chest until I wake up from this dream."

Or get to wherever it is you're taking me.

"I don't mind. All will be well, Billie." His voice caressed her fraying sanity. "I will never let anything happen to you. I promise."

"Yeah, yeah," she grumbled, settling in for however long this lunacy was going to last. She should be furious, petrified, but there was something about hugging him—even if it was to prevent a sudden and hideous drop *sans* parachute. In spite of herself, she felt safe.

Or is he just making you feel that?

The dark thought traced an icy finger up her spine and she tried not to hug him so closely. Which only succeeded in giving gravity the chance to grab at her. She slid a little down his body, barely an inch, gave up trying not to hug him and clung to him like her life depended on it. Which may in fact be the case.

"If you *are* making me think this is all happening, can we move it to somewhere closer to the ground?" she cried out, pressing her cheek harder to his chest.

"Closer to the ground, we can be."

Everything grew still. Her hair fell about her shoulders. She unlocked her legs from around his hips and straightened them. Ground pressed at the bottom of her feet. A part of her mind told her it had always been there. Insisted it.

She shoved herself away from Knight and scanned the darkness around her.

Well, definitely not in Kansas anymore.

She squinted at the bushes and trees and what looked like a cabin lurking behind them.

Or even, it seemed, LA. At least, not *her* part of LA.

"Where are we?" she asked.

"Somewhere safe," Knight growled, walking toward the cabin.

"Safe?" She barked out a laugh. "I'm sorry, but I think the word you mean is ominous."

Without slowing, he tossed her a grin over his shoulder. "Nah. If I meant ominous, there'd be skulls and bones scattered all over the ground."

She blinked, and jerked her stare to her feet.

"And as you can see," his voice mocked her, getting fainter as he walked farther away, "all that's on the ground is—shit."

Shit?

Frowning, she peered harder at the ground. It didn't look like shit. It looked like wild violets and moss and—

"What the hell?"

The startled menace in Knight's murmur tore her focus from the tiny flowers beneath her feet. Something was wrong.

What, apart from the fact you've been abducted by an…an…

Yeah, still had difficulty with the word *angel*.

Lips twisting with a sardonic smile, she closed the distance between them. That sense of needing to be close to him was itching her again, that feeling she was safer with him.

Safer? Or hornier?

He stood at the bottom step leading up to the dark cabin's front porch, staring up at the door. The moon painted pale light over the building, and this close, she could see it was far more modern and structurally sound than she'd first thought. It was the kind of building one could find in the pages of glamorous travel magazines, a cozy Airbnb luxury cabin perfect for the romantic getaway.

Romantic? Really? That's where your head went?

"What's the problem?" she asked. The last thing she needed was to think Knight was a dashing hero worthy of a romance plot.

Instead of answering her, he pulled a phone from the back pocket of his jeans and started swiping his thumb over the screen.

She snorted. "Angels use phones?"

He flicked her an enigmatic look. "They do when they have to call a djinn."

Billie's eyebrows shot up. "A djinn? A genie? Are you sure *you're* not the psycho obsessed with my show and character?"

His teeth flashed at her again as he raised the phone to his ear. "Your show and your character? No." He turned and fixed his attention on the cabin. "James, we've got a problem."

James? The djinn's name was James?

Of course it was.

"Good grief." Rubbing at her arms—wherever he'd brought her, it was colder than LA—she took in her surroundings. She should try to get away. Bolt. While he was talking to James the Genie.

She curled her toes in the soft moss beneath her feet. Running through the dark without shoes wasn't smart.

And staying here with Knight is?

She ran her gaze over his broad back. Maybe. Maybe not.

"Someone's put a ward on the safe house," he said into the phone, dragging a hand through that thick, dark hair of his. Tension radiated from him. The air around him seemed to shimmer, and for a split second Billie swore she saw the massive white wings sprouting from his back again; there and gone before her brain could process the impossible sight.

"I have no clue," he growled, the hand in his hair fisting. "Who knew I was coming here?"

Whatever James said, Knight snarled. "That does me fuck-all good, djinn."

Swallowing, Billie watched him. Someone was not a happy angel.

"No," he said, flicking her another quick glance. "I'm not going to tell you that."

James's answer didn't please him. "Because I had to. It's not Guarded Souls' business. It's a personal situation."

Once again, whatever James said, it made Knight snarl. "Listen, I need to get…a human somewhere safe. A malevolent being, possible another fallen, has done something insanely stupid, dangerously so, and if I don't get her—yes, I said *her*. No, you can't. I just need to get her safe. And I can't because some bastard has put an angel ward on the safe house!"

Billie chewed on her bottom lip. *Destiny's Knight* had covered a menagerie of supernatural and mythological beings in its four-year run, but angels hadn't made an appearance in any episodes so far. Which meant she had nothing to go on regarding the world Knight was from. Were there symbols that could cripple or hamper an angel?

She squinted at the cabin. The night's full moon fought against the heavy clouds in the sky, barely illuminating the building's walls. There didn't seem to be anything painted on them, but who was to say an angel ward would be painted on? For all she knew, it could be scratched into the woodwork. Or spelled out in pebbles on the ground. Hell, one of the techniques her character had implemented to combat a monster-of-the-week had been to smear raw egg yolks across all thresholds.

She wasn't a method actress, but she found the mythology behind some of her character's nonhuman foes and friends fascinating. She researched most of them, creeping herself out sometimes, laughing herself silly at others. She still found the concept of the batsquatch hilarious. As for angels...the only thing she knew of angels was what her mother and aunt had told her over and over like a mantra: God's angels watch over us and do His bidding.

If God—if there really was such a higher being—had sent the snarling, sexy, too-hot-for-words angel in front of her to kidnap her, she really wanted to have a word with Him. He was clearly off His game. Or had a bad sense of humor.

"No!"

Knight's loud growl jerked her attention back to him.

He studied her over his shoulder, fist still in his hair, eyes a shimmering silver light she doubted had anything to do with the hidden moon. A shiver ran up her spine. Her nipples hardened. A warm flutter bloomed in her belly, and lower.

She held that disquieting, nonhuman stare, incapable of looking away. In her throat, her pulse turned into a cannon.

"No," he said again, breaking eye-contact by turning back to the cabin. "I don't need you coming here. Or anyone else from Guarded Souls. I can handle it myself."

James's laugh reverberated through the

phone all the way to where Billie stood.

"Bite me, djinn," Knight said, although the insult held the slightest tinge of mirth.

Shoving his phone back into his pocket, he let out a loud sigh and rubbed at the back of his neck.

"So?" She pinched her thumbnail. "We're going to hang out in the bushes? Or can I just go on inside? This ward that you're talking about? Probably doesn't stop *me* going in, right?"

Another sigh, this one shaky. Put-upon.

"This is a really interesting rescue mission," she said. "Just out of interest."

Knight dropped his hand from his neck. "God, grant me…"

Whatever he wanted God to grant him, he kept it to himself. The muttered words faded to a low groan before he shook his head and turned back to her.

"Okay, change of plans." He closed the distance between them, snaked his arm around her waist and pulled her hard to his body.

"Hey, what—"

His wings appeared.

"Oh great," she muttered, even as her heart slammed into her throat and the junction of her thighs grew hot. "Here we go a—"

Everything turned into a blur.

The sound of massive feathers sliding

together reverberated in her ears, through her body, her soul, and then—just as her brain digested the fact there was no longer cool moss under her feet—she stood on lush carpet. In a split second she'd gone from being outside amongst trees, to inside some kind of building.

But what kind?

"We're here," Knight murmured.

———————

She was meant to be home.

He was told she'd be home. He was *promised* she'd be here.

Promised.

Promised she'd be with *him*. Forever.

He'd given everything—*everything*—for that to be the case.

And that was okay. Because they were meant to be together. She was his Destiny. She breathed for him. She'd said so, in his dreams. More than once.

But that bitch-cow Adelaide Williams had kept him from her. Kept his words of love and devotion from her. Surrounded her with knuckle-dragging, mouth-breathing muscle so he couldn't talk to her. Hold her. Love her.

So he'd done what any man in his situation would do.

He'd sold the only thing of real worth.

His soul.

Willingly gave it up. For her. For *them*.

So where the fuck was she? Why wasn't she home?

He stared at the dark windows of her house.

Since the "transaction," he felt different. Not empty, just…waiting to be filled. By his Destiny.

But it wasn't just that. A low whine filled his head, as if a taut wire stretched behind his eyes, plucked by something cold and hard. Faint at first, the closer he drew to Destiny's home, the louder the whine got. And as it grew louder, an itching burn began to crawl over his skin. It was excruciating in its pain, and yet at the same time, it fed his lust.

Something told him the moment he had her, the moment she was *his*—in body and soul—the whine would disappear and the fire engulfing him would change to one of desirous rapture.

But now the whine screeched, loud and angry.

She wasn't home.

Someone had taken her. The one he'd been warned about.

An angel may come for her, he'd been told as he felt his soul leave his being. *If that is the case, you must deal with him.*

How? he'd asked.

I've equipped you, came the answer, a

soundless voice. *Replaced that which was freely given with the means necessary.*

He had no clue what *the means necessary* meant, but it didn't matter. He would go to his Destiny's home, he would claim her, make her his, and the whine and the fire would stop and they would spend an eternity together. That was the only thing that mattered.

And so he had come to her home.

And she wasn't here.

"Where is she?"

The burn crawling over his skin told him the angel had her.

Deal with him, the soundless voice—a whispered shriek in his head—instructed. *Use that which I've provided you. Before he takes that which belongs to you.*

A wall of fury smashed through him, and he curled his fist. The itching fire flayed his skin. The whine tore at his mind. The air particles around him began to burn.

No one could have his Destiny. She was *his.* Only his. And when he found her, he would—

"Can I help you?"

The male voice behind him—friendly but guarded—made him turn.

A man stood a few feet away, one hand lightly resting on his hip, revealing a glimpse of a gun holster. Cop. His bulk and job would have been imposing to Gilbert, once upon a time. But now…now Gilbert was *more*.

Now he was *Wraif*.

He showed his teeth in a slow smile.

The cop frowned, and the air displaced around him as he closed his fingers tighter around his gun's hilt. "Any reason you're standing here in the dark, buddy? Looking at Ms. Sheridan's house?"

Rage rolled through Wraif. "Don't call her that."

The cop blinked. "Call her—"

"Her name is Destiny!"

Wraif lifted his hands toward the cop and unleashed the burn.

———◆———

This is not smart.

Ha. That was an understatement.

He'd brought the reason for his fall from Heaven to his personal home, the one place no one else—neither human nor otherworldly being—knew about.

Not smart.

Neither is still holding on to her.

The sharp thought slid through his mind, and he pulled his arms from Billie's body. Took a step away from her.

She regarded him for a long moment, expression unreadable.

Her fear hung on the air, tainted it. As did

her anger. And something far more raw and primitive. The very thing he'd been able to tap into when he'd influenced her to kiss him.

Desire.

It threaded around him, tendrils and wisps of an emotion he had little defense against.

Bringing her here was not smart at all.

Here, no one would ever interrupt them.

He remained motionless. Held her steady gaze.

"Where are we?" she asked, her tone as level, as unreadable as her expression. "And don't say somewhere safe. I want specifics. Geographical coordinates if you've got 'em. Longitude and latitude would be helpful."

A slight smile tugged at the corner of his mouth. "Somewhere safe" was exactly the answer he'd been about to give. "My place."

Saying it aloud gave it more weight. Significance. He'd never brought anyone to the home he'd bought on the perimeter of the Angeles National Forest. Had never invited anyone here.

That he even had an earthly residence was a fact his Heavenly brethren would find abhorrent. He'd bought it the day Billie moved to LA from Australia. Until then, he'd existed as any fallen angel did, moving from place to place, asking no one for anything, requiring nothing of anyone.

Not that many of his fellow angels talked to him now. Erah was the only one, and he suspected it had little to do with affection and comradeship, and everything to do with keeping tabs. Nathanial was the angel equivalent of a lone wolf, which always made the *actual* lone wolf at Guarded Souls—wolf shifter, Kitt Newton—chortle when any of the others said it.

Alone and with no family.

Why else had he sought out those not of the human world on Earth since his plummet from Heaven's grace? His position at Guarded Souls allowed him some semblance of human ordinariness, and despite the fact he could influence any human to his will, he preferred the idea of earning a living.

But despite the fact he owned a place to call home, an actual brick-and-mortar residence, he still hadn't been able to bring himself to invite anyone here.

Until now.

Now, he'd brought Billie here.

"My place," he said again, running an objective eye over the room he'd re-substantiated them both in. The living room. Decorated by himself a few years ago in a style he could only describe as "extreme minimalism." A leather lounge suite sat in the middle of the room, flanked by two matching armchairs—all gray in color. On the wall hung a massive television, and in the far corner sat a potted two-meter high Japanese maple he kept alive via not-so-natural means. "It's not much," he said, frowning at the maple, "but it's—"

Something hard thumped against his shoulder, and he went down.

Not from pain or force, but shock.

She'd kicked him? Hit him with something? When he wasn't paying attention?

Leaping back to his feet, he watched her sprint from the room.

Did she have any idea where she was going? "Billie?"

Exasperation laced his shout.

Damn it, she'd lulled him into a false sense of security. He should have known she wouldn't make this easy.

The vibrations on the air, in the floorboards, told him she'd reached the front door.

Closing his eyes, he willed the lock to remain unmoving, no matter how hard she fought with it.

"Billie," he said, shaking his head.

"Goddamn it!" Her frustrated groan floated back to him from the door. "Open up, you goddamn pain in the—"

He materialized behind her and closed his hands around her wrists.

She screamed. Slammed her elbow into his

chest. Smashed her heel down on his foot. Smacked the back of her head into his nose.

This time, however, he was ready for it all.

"Are you done?" he asked. Oh, she was *not* going to like the low chuckle in his voice.

"No, I'm not." She thrashed in his arms. "And you can stop laughing at me!"

"I'm not."

She punched her head back into his face again.

"This will hurt you more than me," he pointed out, keeping his grip on her wrists loose but inescapable.

She writhed in his hold, glaring up at him. "So none of that achieved *anything*?"

"Sorry. No. A human cannot physically injure or wound an angel, no matter *how* much they're channeling Bruce Lee."

She snarled and struggled harder. "Bite me."

"Billie," he intoned, the rapid tattoo of her heart reverberating through his core.

She grew motionless in his arms.

"I promise you," he murmured, caressing her soul with a gossamer thread of calming influence, "I am not the bad guy."

A shaky breath tore from her, and she slumped against his chest. "You can't blame a girl for trying."

He couldn't. And he'd been fooling himself if he'd expected otherwise from her.

Withdrawing the filament of his influence from her will, he released his arms and stepped back.

Slowly, as if waiting for him to attack, she turned and looked up at him. "So, what happens now?"

You kiss me again.

The taboo command whispered through his head. If his influence had still been caressing her will, her lips would be pressed to his now, and her tongue would be lashing against his.

And that's a bad thing?

"Now," he said, taking another step away from her, "you get some sleep and I plan how to deal with Gilbert."

Her eyebrows shot up, disappearing behind the thick auburn curtain of her messy bangs. "Sleep?"

"It's almost four am. Human time."

"Human— Wait." She narrowed her eyes. "So, we're still in the Northern Hemisphere. West Coast time."

"Are you planning on escaping?"

A light gleamed in her eye. Damn it, he shouldn't find it so appealing. "If I am?"

He let out a melodramatic sigh. "Remember how you couldn't unlock the door?"

She dipped her head.

He arched an eyebrow and smiled.

"Really? You can just...what? Make things

happen with your angel mojo?"

Her ferocity would be his undoing. "Really. Now go sleep."

"Yeah, that's not going to happen."

He let out an exasperated groan. "Go read, then."

"What?"

"There's a library down that hall." He pointed to his right.

"Are you trying to win me over the way Beast won over Belle?"

"Who?"

Billie frowned. "You're kidding, right? How much do you know about normal stuff?"

He grinned. "Kidding. I know about normal stuff. I've been watching humanity for many a millennia, and have been personally interacting with your kind for almost as long. I know about normal stuff."

"Phew. I'd hate to think I've been abducted by some kind of weird freak."

He shook his head, even as he perched his ass on the edge of the console table. "I think the word you're looking for is *rescued*."

She arched an eyebrow and crossed her arms. "You don't want to hear the word I'm looking for. And at this point in time, I'm happy with abduction." She rolled her eyes. "I mean, I'm not *happy* you've abducted me, I'm pretty damn pissed about that, but I'm making the assumption angels can't lie, so if you say I'm in serious not-normal-human-stuff danger from Gilbert the stalker, then I believe you. I'm in danger." She stopped, a frown pulling at her eyebrows Nathanial wanted to smooth away with his thumbs. "Angels *can't* lie, right?"

He smiled. "Angels can't lie."

Even fallen ones.

"I promise," he said.

Her gaze searched his, and whatever she saw in his eyes made her relax. A little. He could taste her emotional shift on the air. "Okay," she said.

"Now, will you go sleep?"

He had work to do. Foremost, he needed to find out who exactly had orchestrated the sale of Gilbert Sanders's soul in exchange for Billie's love. He knew it wasn't just a run-of-the-mill crossroad demon. The transaction itself had shuddered the very fabric of existence, which a normal sell-my-soul agreement didn't do. So who had arranged it? Who had sensed Gilbert's obsession with Billie? An obsession so deep and unhinged, he'd give up everything for her? And who had the power and the connections to deliver on such a potent—

"I think I'm just going to curl up on the sofa and watch some TV."

He frowned at Billie's off-handed declaration.

She marched into the living room.

Growling, he followed, just in time to watch her drop onto the sofa facing the television on the wall, tuck her long legs beneath her, and smile at him. "Got Netflix? HBO? I could catch up on *Game of Thrones*."

"The TV isn't plugged in."

He'd never turned the thing on, let alone watched anything on it.

"That's easy to—"

"Wouldn't you prefer to sleep? Or read?"

"Hey, you abducted me. Not my fault I'm not the agreeable victim you were wanting."

If only she knew what level of wanting he experienced when it came to her. Grinding his teeth against the sudden urge to show her, to tap into her base sexual desire for him that he'd already experienced, he shoved himself from the back of the armchair. "Stop saying I abducted you."

"Then let me go."

"Can't do that. You're safer here."

"So this is just about me? Are you *my* guardian angel, or is this a service you offer all humans with stalkers who take it too far? Soul-wise?"

"Let's go with I'm a guardian angel worried about the fact your stalker has been granted…powers beyond a normal soul-selling situation."

You don't think you need to let her know you've been aware of her since before she was born?

"Beyond normal soul-selling... Y'know, I'm still halfway convinced this whole thing is an elaborate prank. I mean, Joe Abbott, *Destiny's Knight's* showrunner, did *not* think it was funny when I replaced his Nutella with Vegemite. He swore he'd get me back. This *is* kinda his level of revenge. Some of the pranks he pulls on set are—"

"This isn't a prank, Billie." She needed to understand that.

She chewed on her bottom lip and pinched her thumbnail. Did she know she did that? When she was feeling uncertain?

"Can I call Adelaide?" she asked. Concern filled the question. "She'll be freaking out by now, wondering where I am, and I'd hate for her to be worried. She's trying to kick a pretty nasty nicotine habit. I don't want to be the reason she opens another packet of cigarettes."

Adelaide Williams already had the early stages emphysema, but neither she nor Billie knew that.

"It's taken care of."

She blinked. "What does that mean?"

He swallowed and rubbed at the back of his neck. Kade had a unique talent for mimicry. Nathanial had asked him to call Billie's agent and, using Billie's voice, tell the woman she was okay and the cops were taking care of the situation.

"It means, you don't have to worry about Adelaide Williams. And if it helps, I can cure her of her addiction."

"Whoa." She gazed up at him. "Are you serious? I've been petrified she's going to get lung cancer, and I've wanted her to quit for years."

"I *am* serious. If it's important to you, I'll make certain she will be o—"

She threw herself from the sofa, wrapped her arms around his neck and smacked her lips to his.

He froze.

So did she.

"Shit," she muttered, jerking away.

The back of her knee collided with the armchair's seat and, another shit bursting from her, she tumbled sideways.

He caught her. Righted her. The warm softness of her skin branded into his palms, the soft inhalation of her gasp flayed his sanity, and before he could stop himself, he smoothed a hand up her arm and cupped the side of her face.

He'd experienced a lifetime of being aware of her, an eternity, and here they were.

For a fleeting moment, she closed her eyes and pressed her cheek to his palm—and then she stepped backward, avoiding the armchair this time.

She studied him, the little pulse in her neck beating like a frenzied butterfly. "I'm sorry. I didn't mean...I shouldn't have—" She stopped, eyes narrowing. "Did you do that? Did you just use your Jedi—your *angel* powers to make me kiss you?"

"No." The denial rumbled deep in his chest. "You did that of your own accord."

"Really?"

"Yes. I promised you, I would never make you do that a—"

She closed the tiny distance between them, tangled her fingers in his hair, and crushed his lips with hers.

He opened to her without hesitation. Instinctually. As if he'd been the willing recipient of her kisses for his entire life.

Her tongue stroked over his, and unlike the kiss they'd shared outside her house, this one destroyed him. The kiss on her pathway had been a product of his influence. Yes, he'd tapped into her visceral attraction to him, but he'd been responsible for it happening. This kiss...

He'd had nothing to do with this kiss. And he was lost to it.

Pleasure unlike any he believed possible rushed through his existence. His head swam and, as she drew herself up onto tiptoe and deepened the kiss, he fisted his hands in the back of her tank top and hauled her body harder against his.

She moaned, the raw sound vibrating through her chest, feeding a need for her beyond his comprehension.

If his only purpose for being created was this one moment, this one honest, willing kiss, then his existence was served well.

But it's not. You know that. You know why you were created, and it has nothing to do with this.

Billie tore her lips from his and twisted out of his arms. "Shit! *Again.*"

The soft mutter twisted a cold fist in his heart,

He stood motionless. Studied her.

"Shit," she whispered, pulling at her thumbnail as her gaze flicked all over the room, the floor, everywhere but to him. "I'm sorry. I shouldn't have... Damn it!"

Shuffling her feet, she scrunched up her face. "That was...whoa, I mean, seriously... Kissing you is like kissing raw sexual energy and electricity and...and...whoa."

He remained still. Immobilized by the fear she was about to accuse him of influencing her again.

He'd faced down some of the worst Hell spawn birthed by Lucifer; he'd fought in brutal wars no mortal mind could comprehend. But right now, the possibility Billie might think he'd compelled her to kiss him robbed him of movement. Action.

All he could do was wait.

And hope…

"I think…" She scratched the side of her nose, her eyes flicking to him for a split second before dropping to the floor. "I think I *will* try to catch some sleep after all."

He dipped his head in a single nod. It was for the best. He had no business allowing her to kiss him, or kissing her in return—wanting to do *more* than kiss her in return—and he *did* have work to do.

He couldn't concentrate on finding the fallen responsible for this situation with Billie close to him. Being in the same building was stretching his control as it was, distracting him.

"Your room is down the hall, second on the right."

She cocked an eyebrow even as she pulled a shaky breath. "*My* room? Been planning this for long? Are you *sure* it's Gilbert I need to be worried about?"

He snorted out a laugh and rolled his eyes. "The room you can use while you are here."

She chewed her bottom lip and shuffled her feet again.

"Consider it your private space. I will not

enter it without your express permission."

"Like a vampire?"

He pictured Kade. The thought of Guarded Souls' owner, a 3,000-year-old vampire at Billie's bedroom door, with his brooding masculinity and timeless sensuality, made his teeth ache. Something dark and ancient snaked through him.

Jealousy?

"Like an *angel*," he answered, with a small dip of his head. "We winged ones cannot lie, remember."

Eyes narrowing, she plucked at her thumbnail. "Fair enough. Any chance you might have left some clothes for me in that room? Seeing as I'm…" She flicked a glance down her body.

He didn't do the same. Her current attire—the black tank top and boxer shorts she'd been wearing when she'd invited him into her home—taunted him. It was branded in his brain, his consciousness. His very soul. Indelible and inescapable.

"You'll find spare clothes in the closet."

Her eyebrows disappeared behind her fringe again.

"Some of my older clothes," he clarified. Hell, why did the image of her in his old PJs suddenly render him on fire? "Items I no longer require."

Her lips twitched. "I'm not sure we've reached that stage of the relationship, Mr. Knight, me wearing your clothes, but seeing as I have no real choice…"

She turned and walked from the living room.

He moved his stare to the dark television screen and kept it there. Safer that way.

She lingered on the air though, taunting him, teasing his senses. An angel's senses were heightened, the pinnacle of conditioning and creation. At that moment, he'd give his left arm for the less-than-effective sensory development of a mere human.

The second door on the right down the hallway opened, and he stiffened. "Wilhelmina?" he called. His reflection stared back at him from the television's screen. His own eyes judged him, mocked him. "Don't try to escape."

"You're taking all the fun out of this abduction, Mr. Knight." Her reproach floated back to him from the hallway.

He grimaced around a low laugh and rubbed a hand over the back of his neck. "Not an abduction, Billie," he corrected.

"In that case, I expect poached eggs, avocado, and Vegemite on toast for breakfast tomorrow morning." He smiled at the laughter in the her retort. "And contact my masseuse.

For some reason, I feel like I've been put through the wringer."

"Good night, Billie."

"Good night, Nathanial."

He closed his eyes.

His name. She'd finally said his name.

If she knew how much it affected him, she'd likely make a deal with Lucifer *herself* to get as far away from him as she could.

Seconds of silence stretched for an eternity before Billie closed the door.

Eyes still closed, he felt her moving around the spare room, exploring it, before the springs of the mattress told him she'd climbed into bed.

"Enough." He barred his mind to her. Shut down the craving to connect with her.

Lowering himself into the armchair she'd collided with, he concentrated on Gilbert Sanders instead.

Searched for him.

With any human, there was a certain ebbing and flowing of their impact on existence, an impact angels could tap into if required. But Gilbert's impact had shifted. He was hard to find.

Worryingly so.

It shouldn't be this difficult to locate him, even without his—

"There," he muttered at the hint of a hazy presence. "Found you."

Wisps of the man hung on the temporal plane, faint and fraying.

A cold tension bloomed in Nathanial's chest. The willing sale of Gilbert's soul had morphed him into something beyond human, which was *not* normal for such a transaction. In fact, the remnants of his human existence barely tinged the Order of Actuality.

Concentrating harder, he snagged one of the wisps with his mind, and—cloaking his own presence—melded his consciousness with it.

—*musthaveherlustherburningupburningmust haveherfindhermust*—

A scream ripped through the air. High and shocked.

He recoiled, tearing himself from the turbulent, licentious chaos of Gilbert's subconscious. Flashes of his brief second joined to the man's mind lashed at him, thick and hot and insidious, and he clawed at his scalp.

What the *hell* was that?

Nothing like you've ever experienced before.

Clammy ice crawled over him, tainted with depravity, obsession and…more. A burning chill, at once primordial and newborn.

His stomach lurched. Thankfully he hadn't eaten in over a week, otherwise he suspected everything in his gut would be expelled from his body in a violent gush and on the floor now.

"Knight?"

He jerked upright in the armchair at the sound of Billie's voice, swiping at his mouth.

Can't let her see you like this.

"You okay?"

She rounded the side of the chair, worry etched on her face.

He ground his teeth. The sight of her wearing his old sweatpants battered his sanity. She was too human, too easy to break, to wound. Too fragile and precious.

Too defenseless.

Protect her.

Scrubbing at the back of his neck, he frowned. "Of course I'm okay."

She frowned back. "So you just randomly scream for no reason then? It's a thing you do?"

"Scream? I didn't..."

The earlier wail, the one he'd heard as he'd torn himself from Gilbert's existence thread in the temporal plane, came back to him.

His scream.

He swiped at his mouth again and rose to his feet, almost knocking into Billie.

She scurried back a step, exasperation replacing the worry on her face. "Sure, I'll get out of your road."

He needed... He needed...

Help.

Shit.

"Hey."

A strong, warm hand closed around his arm, and he hissed, flinching from the touch.

"Knight." Billie frowned, her grip tightening. "Talk to me. You look like you've seen a ghost. Can you? I mean, can angels see ghosts?"

He dropped his stare to where her fingers pressed to his skin. Contact. Her body to his.

Her flesh to his.

Destiny… My Destiny…

His. To kiss whenever *he* wanted. She was *his.* He'd sold his—

He reeled away from her, on fire and enveloped in ice at the same time.

"Knight?" His name fell from her in a shaky whisper. Fear laced the sound.

Knight. Nathanial Knight. His name was Nathanial Knight. He was an angel, not…

Gilbert.

The memory of what she looked like to the man, how Gilbert hungered for her, assaulted Nathanial, like molten iron searing into raw flesh.

The connection. Melding with the now soulless man. It had…had…

He shuddered, skin crawling, a sour tang filling his mouth.

How was he to locate the man if he couldn't seek out the wisps of his threads? How else was he to know where Gilbert Sanders was if being infected by the man's unhinged lust for Billie was the result?

"I will slap the hell out of you if you don't tell me what's going on?" Billie growled to his right.

He flicked her a glance—and gasped as a tsunami of craven lust smashed through him. *Gilbert's* lust.

Closing his eyes, he drew a deep breath. Human behavior, to be sure, but it grounded him. Fought against the taint of Gilbert in his being.

Releasing it, he opened his eyes again.

Looked at Billie.

A wave of desire swept through him, but *his*. The one he'd wrestled with for a lifetime. Not Gilbert's. His own.

"I'm okay, Billie," he said, keeping his voice calm. "I'm sorry I startled you. It was just a…"

Just a what?

"An angel thing," he finished.

Her frown deepened. "Are you sure?"

He nodded.

She studied him for a second. "I *have* pointed out this is a very weird abduction, right?"

"Rescue," he said with a smile.

She chuckled. "Right. See you in the morning."

She left again, glancing back at him once before making her way to her room.

He didn't move until the door to the room closed once more, and then he slumped into the armchair, squeezed his eyes shut, and released the restraint on his mind.

Erah, he called silently. *Brother, I need you.*

Chapter Four

"First things first," Billie muttered, rubbing her palms on her thighs. "Getting out of here."

But that kiss…

"Getting out of here," she repeated, fisting the soft material of Knight's sweatpants as she studied the windows of the room.

Seriously, that kiss, though.

"Is the *reason* to get with the getting out of here."

Crossing the room, she parted the gauzy curtains and tugged at the window's lock.

Nothing. Not even a hint of a movement.

Gritting her teeth, she tried the lock again.

Nope. It didn't budge.

"Damn it."

Outside, clouds streamed across the dark sky, playing peekaboo with the fat moon. Way off in the distance, a faint white glow rose up from the horizon. LA? Or somewhere else?

If it was somewhere else, how did they get there so fast?

"And if it *is* LA," she muttered, "getting this far away from it in a matter of seconds isn't fast? Or freaky?"

She sighed and pressed her forehead to the glass, studying the glow for a few moments before checking out the dark ground on the other side of the window.

Well, at least she now knew they *were* in a house, an actual house, and not in some weird, floating-in-the-sky/other-dimension type thing.

"Huh, always looking for the silver lining, Bill."

A soft laugh fell from her. There was no denying the whole thing was *beyond* weird, but she had two options for dealing with it. One, accept she really was caught up in some kind of otherworldly situation, or two, accept the fact she'd lost her mind at some point and was probably tripping on medication in a padded cell right now. And while the first option was borderline insane, it was better than the last.

"Still not going to sit around and wait for whatever's about to happen next though," she grumbled, pushing away from the window and moving to the one next to it.

We don't want to think some more about that

kiss? Maybe go out there and ask for another one?

"No, we don't." She fought with the curtain—stupid floaty thing—and grabbed at the lock. "And no, we don't."

The lock didn't move.

"Damn it," she repeated, twisting around to slump against the wall.

Sliding down it, she hit the floor with a soft thud and, wrapping her arms around her knees, glared at the room.

As far as prisons went, it was cozy. If Knight had decorated it, he had good taste. Just like the living room, it was understated class, with a muted color scheme of grays and whites. The bed was massive, as was the mirror on the opposite wall. In the closet, along with the sweatpants she'd already nabbed, was an array of jeans, chinos, and shirts. Knight had a thing for neutral colors in his wardrobe. Was that an angel thing? Was there a uniform for when those of his kind wandered around here on Earth amongst the mortals?

The kiss?

She huffed into her fringe.

Okay, sure. She wasn't going anywhere. Not at the moment, at least. May as well contemplate The Kiss.

She knew this one had been different. Nothing like the kiss she'd given Nathanial while under his...angel/Jedi influence, the kiss in the living room had utterly shaken her to her very core. While the kiss he'd elicited from her back at her house had somehow been tinged with an out-of-body lightness, like the whole thing had been filtered through a misty lens, *this* one had been vivid and sharp in its clarity. There'd been no confusion or hesitation or delirium.

Overwhelmed by the news he could cure Adelaide of her nicotine addiction, she'd instantly regressed to the behavior of an excited little girl and kissed him without thought.

But it had ignited something in her. That quick and impulsive connection of lips had awaken in her a desire for more, a *need* for more, and when he'd sworn he'd had nothing to do with that brief kiss, well, that need had urged—no, *propelled* her to kiss him again.

To truly kiss him.

Of her own accord.

For her own desire.

For her own…

"Lust?"

She shoved herself to her feet.

From the second Nathanial Knight had smiled at her through the camera of her CCTV screen, she'd accepted she was sexually attracted to him. The second he'd crossed her threshold, the second she'd breathed him in, touched his hard body with her fingers, felt his skin warm hers…yeah, sexual attraction was an understatement. But that last kiss… She'd never had a kiss rock her to the core like that.

Not even her producer—who'd popped her sexual-exploration cherry in more ways than one—had turned her veins to molten rivers of carnal hunger.

And yet it was more than that. That kiss…there was a promise to it, a whole new existence.

A glimmer of something beyond sexual attraction.

A hope of something…deeper. More profound.

Significant.

"And that's enough thinking of the kiss." She had to get out of here, before she completely lost all sense of reality and decided it was possible to fall in love with an angel. Rubbing her palms on the thighs of Knight's sweatpants again, she hurried to the bed. The pillows on it were big and fluffy. One of those pressed to the window would surely muffle the sound of the glass breaking when she smashed her shoulder against it.

She tested the pillows, weighed them against each other, and selected the one she liked the most.

You know this is lunacy, right?

Yep. But to hell with doing nothing. She

was not the do-nothing kind.

If she was, she wouldn't have up and moved to the US on a whim to see what else life had to offer when she was eighteen. She'd most likely still be working at the deli in her local supermarket, wondering *what if?*

Of course, if you were still at the deli, Gilbert the Stalker wouldn't even know you existed, so he wouldn't have become obsessed with you, wouldn't have sold his soul to the devil to get you, and you wouldn't now be cast in the role of damsel in distress with a sexier than legally allowed angel as your unlikely savior.

"Oh boy." Yeah, this situation…

"Time to get out of it," she muttered. "Before I go completely crazy."

She'd get out, away from the unnerving allure of Nathanial Knight and his equally unnerving story, and get her arse to the nearest police station. Tell them about Gilbert, leave out the abduction-by-angel part, and call Adelaide.

Yeah, that's a plan. A sane plan. Let's get on it.

Hugging the pillow to her chest, she crossed to the door and—wincing at the possibility of it squeaking—inched it open.

Listened.

Knight's deep voice—like distant thunder—wafted back to her from the living room. Who was he talking to? The djinn he'd mentioned earlier? Himself?

Voices in his head?

Didn't matter. The fact there was no other voice was enough to let her know he was still alone. He may be an angel, and phenomenally sexy, and incomprehensibly the best kisser in existence, but that didn't mean he wasn't loopy, too.

Adding a precautionary cringe to her wince, she closed the door, tested it really was closed—and then realized she had no way of stopping him from coming into the room at the sound of breaking glass, muffled by a pillow or not.

"Damn it," she whispered yet again.

Her mother would want to wash her blasphemous mouth out with soap.

She scanned the room. Thanks to Knight's affection for minimalism, there wasn't a bureau or dresser she could use as a barricade at the door.

Of course. Had she really thought escaping from an angel would be easy?

Tugging at her thumbnail, she frowned. Maybe if she pulled all the bedding from the mattress and piled it against the door? It wouldn't slow him down for long, but it could be enough.

Cringe and wince firmly back in place, she yanked the duvet, other pillows, and sheets from the bed and heaped them against the door.

She studied her handiwork. Hardly a fortified barrier, but then, she didn't have much to work with. "It'll have to do."

Retrieving her preferred glass-smashing pillow from the now naked bed, she crossed to the window, slid the curtains open, and checked outside again.

It didn't look that far down to the ground. A few feet.

It's also dark. What if there're rocks? You're not wearing any shoes.

Grinding her teeth, she took a few steps away from the window and pressed the pillow to the curve of her shoulder.

She'd seen stunt doubles on the show do this kind of thing many times, throw themselves through a window. She herself had practiced the move—under the guidance of the show's stunt coordinator—more than once, in a desire to do her own stunts, until the studio's insurance agency stepped in and vetoed the idea. Of course, that had been prop glass, and there'd been no need to try to hide the whole routine from an angel in the other room who may or may not be delusional, so there was that, but...

"Just do it, woman," she growled, pressing the pillow closer to her shoulder as she backed as far away from the window as the room would allow. Her heels nudged the duvet on the floor. She flicked them a look, and then glared at the window. Swallowed. "Just suck it up and do it."

She sprinted at the window.

And hit the brakes a few feet from her target.

What the *hell* was she thinking?

Her feet tangled beneath her. Arms pinwheeling, the pillow a useless projectile now heading for the floor, she let out a strangled *eep*.

Idiot. Idi—

Her right foot snagged her left ankle and she slammed into the floor, shoulder first, sans pillow.

Something cracked, splintered. Pain blasted through her shoulder, up into her neck, down her arm.

"Fuck!" she cried, grabbing at the sudden inferno in her shoulder, even as her momentum continued to carry her in an awkward slide across the hardwood. "Oh fuck, that hurts!"

And then the very air around her displaced, and she was in strong arms, being lifted from the floor, Nathanial's hard, warm chest pressed to her side, his lips pressed to her temple as he murmured in that language she couldn't understand.

Warmth flooded her. Flowed through her shoulder. The pain intensified, as if fighting for its survival, and then—nothing.

No pain. No numbness.

Nothing.

Nathanial's low murmuring stopped. His lips caressed her temple for a heartbeat longer, and then her feet were returned to the floor.

"Wh-what…" She gaped up at him, cupping a shoulder she swore was broken a second ago. "How…"

He studied her, expression unreadable. Except for a twitch in his jaw, as a muscle there tightened. "How does it feel?"

She frowned at the calm control in his voice. Or maybe she trembled? The way he looked at her, the way her body strained toward him…

Swallowing, she rolled her shoulder, keeping her palm on the joint. It moved beneath her hand with fluid ease. No pain sheared through her at the action. None. "It's…it's okay."

The words left her on a husky breath.

He stood motionless, regarding her.

Behind him, the air shimmered. His wings. There, but not there.

She frowned, returning her stare to his face. "Did you know what I was doing? That I was trying to…" Heat filled her cheeks.

"No. But when I felt your shoulder break, I suspected."

"You felt it break? In your own shoulder, you mean?"

He inclined his head in a single nod.

"Okay, that's…kind of daunting. Have you always been able to feel what I feel?"

A faint frown tugged at his eyebrows. If she hadn't been staring at him so hard, she would have missed it. "No. This is a new development."

"How new?"

"Since you kissed me of your own free will."

Oh boy.

His eyes dropped to her lips, and then he turned and walked to the door.

"Nathanial?"

He paused, his shoulders tensing.

"Thank you."

"Don't mention it."

She chewed on her lip.

"There's no barrier now, Billie," he said over his shoulder.

Her heart thumped up into her throat. "The doors and windows…"

"Will open," he finished, before walking through the door. Out of the room. Out of her sight.

Frowning, she turned from the empty doorway. The curtains still hung parted on the window she'd selected to make her dramatic escape. The night beyond sat waiting, a lighter hue smudging on the eastern horizon.

Rubbing at a shoulder that should have been

a screaming world of self-inflicted agony but instead felt like it had just experienced the best massage of its existence, she crossed to the window.

Touched her fingertips on the glass.

And then turned away.

A soft laugh burst from her and, walking to the bed, she flopped onto it face-first.

He trusted her, Nathanial trusted her.

She would do the same for him.

After all, what kind of angel couldn't a person trust?

And let's be serious, there is that kiss to think about...

So yep, she was staying put. Insanity at its highest, but the only course of action that made any real sense.

"God help me," she mumbled into the duvet.

Erah either didn't hear him or chose not to respond.

Most likely the latter.

Pacing the living room, Nathanial raked his hands through his hair.

The situation was escalating rapidly, and it seemed he was now operating blind. There was no way he could risk tapping into Gilbert's threads again, not after the way the man's unhinged, depraved lust for Billie had affected him. And the only option he had on his own to track Gilbert's location was via the wisps of his existence.

With that process denied him, and his brother angel silent to him…

"Fuck."

The curse fell from him, barely a breath but louder than a shout in his soul. It wasn't that angels were forbidden to use profanity. They weren't. There was little considered to be the conception of man that was forbidden to angels. Why would beings of divine creation be tempered by anything so lowly? But the ability to do so was deeply hobbled in *their* creation.

Think it, yes. Any and every word and term considered a vulgar expletive was available to his thoughts. But to utter it…well, that required stupendous levels of emotional force.

"Stupendous levels of emotion" almost came close to summing up his current state.

He was, to put it more accurately, a fucking wreck.

Anyone at Guarded Souls would help him, but the selling of a soul was angel work, as was cleaning up its mess.

Closing his eyes, he rubbed at his shoulder. A dull ache throbbed in the joint, like his arm had been ripped from its socket and rudely shoved back in a lifetime ago.

Billie's pain.

Pain was a new experience for him, at least pain of this type. Human pain. Yes, other angels could wound him, kill him, but a human could not. The fact he could feel Billie's pain as it happened...

So many unanswered questions.

The pain, the silence from Erah, the unknown orchestrator behind Gilbert's perverse elevation, the unexpected absorption of Gilbert lust, the kiss...

"Fuck," he ground out.

Once again, the word tore at him, like a whip dipped in acid.

It didn't, however, lessen the memory of Billie's lips on his, the honest and willing hunger in her kiss as she sought out his tongue, demanded it with her own.

Dropping into the nearest armchair, he closed his eyes.

An eternity.

That's how long he'd known his existence wasn't as simple as it should be. An angel's purpose was not complex; do what you were created for.

An eternity of doing just that, and then, eons ago...

A soft sigh left him.

He'd first become aware of the force of life that would one day be Billie Sheridan 300 years ago. The faintest ripple in an endless ocean, a schism in the light of future existence, drew him. He investigated, despite it being suggested by his fellow angels that to do so would anger God.

The ripple grew stronger as time passed. The light grew brighter. Until he could feel it in his very core.

He had no clue what it was, who it was, this light. But he couldn't ignore it. There was something to it, something…profound. Or was it more that it somehow made him want something beyond his simple purpose?

An angel should never crave anything more than that which they already possessed and knew. That was the Word and the Way. But that light…it streamed into him, in tiny filaments that became a wave. Flowed into him. Filled him.

He tried to deny it. Tried to ignore it.

Turned his energies to the battles for which God had created him. With renewed vigor, he fought the malevolence sent by the darkest of them all. Rendered more than one invulnerable foe nonexistent in battle. Tore apart evil, hunted down darkness.

And the whole time, the intriguing light flowed into him. Challenged him.

Why was this light, this force, there? Why did he feel it, why had it come to him, when he was forbidden to acknowledge it?

What was it? *Who* was it?

And why did it make him question himself? Begin to question his purpose?

No answers, none, only more warnings from his fellow angels to stay away from it, to reject it, shun it.

No reason was given why, just the warning. *This is not for your concern, brother.* Over and over. *This is not for your concern. Turn away, brother. Deny it.*

And he tried. He truly did.

It was not his purpose, not his reason for being.

He tried to forget it.

God knows, he tried.

Until 300 years later, when the light became the promise of existence, one whispered to the deepest corners of his boundless soul: Wilhelmina Sheridan.

When he realized it was a human soul—not yet even born—that drew him, he swore to refute its allure.

Swore to uphold his true purpose.

And once more, he tried.

Poured every molecule of his being into denying what drew him.

Tried. For twenty-three years.

Until Erah found him in agony over his internal battle, and in an act of weakness, Nathanial told him everything.

Erah had regarded him with silent contemplation, studied him, wings tucked, expression indecipherable. And then, lips curling a little, he cupped his hand behind Nathanial's head and whispered in his ear—

"Fuck me, Feathers."

The deep voice, laced with laughter, jolted Nathanial to his feet.

Wings snapping wide, fist balling, he stared—stunned—at the man standing before him.

Mirth twinkled in James Hastin's black eyes as he raked a look over Nathanial. "You look like shite. What've you been doin'?"

The breath burst from Nathanial in a rush. Shaking his head, he relaxed his fists and scrubbed at his face. "How the hell did you know where I am?"

No one knew where they were. Not even Billie.

James grinned. "Djinn, mate. Remember? I think about something I want, and bam—it's either with me, or I'm with it. Well, sort of."

Nathanial frowned at the djinn. Or rather, his image. James *appeared* as if he was there in the living room, but he wasn't. "I hate how you do that."

"So you've said. I can't help being awesome. Can I assume you've tucked the wings away?"

"You can." Rolling his shoulders, Nathanial

winced at the sharp stab of pain sinking into the right one. "What *are* you doing here?"

Who knew where James really was? Likely back at the Guarded Souls offices in LA, but then again, it *was* James. He could be in Greenland.

The djinn let out a low grunt. "We got a problem. And by 'we,' I mean you."

Yeah. Add it to the list. "And that is?"

"The corpse of a cop has just been found in LA."

"So?"

"Outside the home of one Wilhelmina Sheridan."

All the heat left the room. Someone, a cop, had died near Billie's home.

Rhames? Surely not. Nathanial had instructed him to leave.

Hadn't he?

James narrowed his eyes. "If I'm not mistaken, that was the woman you asked Kade to mimic in a call to someone named Adelaide Williams, yes? Wilhelmina Sheridan? Although you called her Billie."

"How?" The single word scratched at Nathanial's dry throat.

"How what?"

"How did the cop die?"

James swiped at his mouth. The distaste etching his face made Nathanial's gut clench.

James rarely looked anything but bemused. "Burnt to death. The residue energy emanating from the corpse says he was set alight while still alive. He was a big bastard, too, before his death."

Detective Rhames.

It was Nathanial's turn to rub at his mouth. He'd *felt* Rhames's soul. It had been pure and strong. The detective had been a good man. True and honest, someone who loved his wife and children unconditionally. Who went to work every day with the sole purpose of making the world a better place for them, and for society. And now he was dead.

But why?

He frowned at James. "Why does anyone at Guarded Souls know about this? Humans are killed all the time. What flagged the agency?"

"It wasn't a natural fire, Feathers."

Nathanial's throat tightened.

James—rarely serious, even when facing down all manner of threat—studied Nathanial with a steady look. "It pinged Nim's internal radar. Kade and Christen got there as soon as they could but it was too late to save him." He shook his head. "There's nothing natural about this one, and we figured, given the location of the attack, the proximity to this Sheridan woman, you'd want to know."

They'd figured right.

Clawing at the back of his neck, Nathanial closed his eyes and searched for Rhames's existence in the ethereal plane.

Nothing.

No, wait…

He concentrated harder, searching.

There. A weak cry. An echo. Faint and wretched and tortured.

Bile churned in the back of Nathanial's throat. The detective hadn't just been burnt alive, his soul had almost been incinerated from existence.

Impossible.

"You're tapping into the plane?"

Opening his eyes, he sighed at James, who still studied him with that out-of-character solemn look. "Yeah."

Of all those on the payroll at Guarded Souls Security and Protection, Nathanial was the only angel, the only one able to slip into the ethereal plane of existence to determine the living status of a human. It came in handy often. Those who engaged the services of the agency didn't know the nonhuman state of the team, but as unaware as they were, they always appreciated their supernatural abilities.

"Is the cop who you think he is?" James asked. "The reason for the dire light in your eyes?"

"He is."

An image of Rhames smiling at him flared in Nathanial's mind. His chest ached. He'd left the cop with a gossamer line of influence still threaded through his will, enough for Nathanial to get away from Billie's place, and to ensure the authorities didn't notice she was gone. He'd also ensured that influence had left Rhames in a happy place, not a confrontational one.

You left him vulnerable. He wouldn't have been prepared for any kind of assault.

Guilt snaked into Nathanial's gut, coiling around the unease already there.

The death of an innocent human was now on his hands. Was this part of the unspoken reason he'd been instructed to forget Billie Sheridan existed eons ago?

"That sucks," James said. Regret replaced the serious frown on his face. Another new expression Nathanial had never seen on the djinn before. "Wilhelmina Sheridan has something to do with what's going on, yes? What's that mean for you?"

Nathanial cupped the back of his head in both hands, stare locked on the floor.

Should he tell James? Fill him in on Gilbert? The sale of a human's soul wasn't the normal situation Guarded Souls dealt with, regardless of the agency's name, but then, nor was it normal fallen angel territory. Fallen angels were meant to exist amongst humans but not concern themselves with such trivial matters, under implied threat of punishment.

Nothing trivial about this, though, is there? Even ignoring who Gilbert sold his soul for.

Damn it, he needed to speak to Erah. Whatever Gilbert had become, he didn't want to risk the lives of his friends, and the melting pot of nonhumans who worked at Guarded Souls were now just that—friends.

"Nath?"

He lifted his head at James's soft voice. The djinn rarely called him anything but Feathers, and sometimes—when he was in a particularly irritating mood—Flappy. The only time *Nath* was uttered by James, or anyone on the Guarded Souls team, for that matter, was when things were truly worrying. Which meant he'd heard it a grand total of twice.

"Do you want our help?" James's image shimmered. Not a lot, but just enough for Nathanial to remember he wasn't actually there. "I can round everyone up. Get them all there within—"

Nathanial shook his head. "This is angel business. There won't be anything you can do."

"So you think it's another fallen that's responsible?"

"It seems so. Or at least, they are involved in

some way."

Surprise flittered across James's face. Uncertainty did the same in his green eyes. "I thought we knew all the fallen?"

Nathanial had started a database of all the fallen angels residing amongst man when he was cast out. He'd shared that list with Guarded Souls during his second month on the team. As a show of goodwill, and as a contingency in case anything happened to him.

Letting out a ragged sigh, he raked a hand through his hair. "I thought we did as well. But this situation, this soul transaction…" He shook his head again. "This one is…different."

"If you find yourself up the proverbial creek, wish for a paddle and I'll deliver."

A low chuckle bubbled up Nathanial's throat. "Genie jokes? You must be worried about me, Jimmy. I'm touched."

James flashed a wicked grin. "In the head, Feather." His image shimmered again, and for a split second he appeared to flick someone else a quick look. Another member of the Guarded Souls team? Where exactly was he? "Touched in the head."

Nathan laughed again. "If you were here right now, I'd kick your ass."

"You'd try. I've got a massive set of clippers, though. Those wings of yours…" He wriggled his eyebrows, bent himself into a deep bow, and disappeared.

Revealing the angel lounging in the armchair opposite Nathanial.

"Hello, brother." Ice-blue eyes locked on him, iridescent with the full force of divine creation and grace. "You've been trying to contact me, yes?"

Burning the cop alive had fed him. Somehow.

He still didn't know how he'd burned him.

The man had been standing in front of him, talking to him. Had said her name, his Destiny's *other* name, the one she used to *pretend* she wasn't who she really was, and at the sound of that name (*Ms. Sheridan*), something in him had cracked, like a fissure in the bowels of the Earth. The *him* he'd once been (*Gilbert*) fell into the abyss, and the fire crawling over the him he now was burned the air between him and the cop.

He'd watched the cop shriek a silence scream. Watched smooth skin blister, blacken, melt...

A voice from a dying part of his mind screamed as well, the part belonging to the him he used to be (*Gilbert*). That voice begged him to undo it all. To take it all back. Oh God, take it back!

But the fire engulfed that pathetic plea as ferociously as it engulfed the cop.

Destroyed it.

Used it.

And fed him.

Empowered him.

And the more the cop burned, the more he became aware of a tugging sensation in the void once filled by his soul.

A dark, hungry tug eager for him (*Wraif*) to come.

As the charred lump of flesh and bone that had once been the foolish cop smoldered at his feet, he closed his eyes and gave himself over to the tug.

—*waitingforyouwraifwantyouneedyoucometo mewraiffindme*—

Destiny.

His Destiny. He needed to go to her. The angel had her. He needed to take her back from the angel.

You need to be stronger, the soundless voice guiding and helping him whispered in his head. *To face down the angel, to take back that which belongs to you, you need to be stronger.*

Fury roared through Wraif. He stared at the blackened corpse at his feet, seeking out its energy.

Nothing. It was all gone. Depleted.

He balled his fists, sinking his nails into his

palms. No! How would he rescue his Destiny if he—

You know how, the soundless voice chided.

Loosening his fists, Wraif shook out his shoulders and laughed.

He did. Of course he did.

———+———

Erah smiled. As relaxed and calm as always.

"You look frazzled, brother." He settled back deeper in the armchair, and threaded his fingers behind his head. His long blond hair— normally braided and contained with a beaten gold band—slipped loose over his shoulders, like a waterfall of pale honey. "What ails you?"

Nathanial kept his own expression blank, even as a wave of charged energy swept through him, heightening...*everything*. When in close proximity, angels fed off each other's force, a natural and automatic defense system they had no control over. It ensured one angel was never more powerful than another, their force ever flowing between them. And if one angel went down, surrounding angels were still charged with equal vitality. A divine reinforcement, as such, to aid their strength.

Nathanial had not drawn on the potency of another angel in centuries. Erah's force flowed into him now, igniting sensations long denied him.

Sensations, and a raw current of unfathomable might.

"Feel better?" A soft laugh danced on Erah's question. "Had your fill yet?"

Nathanial swallowed. His body thrummed. His soul did the same. And yet, it wasn't enough. How could it be? He'd been denied for so long, he hadn't realized how starved he was, how thirsty, like a man suddenly allowed to breathe again, or a fish thrown back into the ocean after hours left in the sun on the beach.

Sucking in a steadying breath, he allowed his eyes to close for a brief second, savoring the rush, and then returned his attention to Erah.

Erah's blue gaze held his, enigmatic. Impossible to read. But a slow smile played with the corners of Erah's lips, and he leaned forward, resting his elbows on his denim-clad knees. "I have miss you, brother."

The declaration stirred a deep longing in Nathanial's core. Of all his fellow angels, Erah was the one he'd allied with the most. Both created for battle, both charged with the protection of Heaven's gates, both ready to die for each other.

Until the light that was Billie…

The thrumming in his body and core faded, replaced instead with an urge to hurry to her room, to check on her.

He couldn't. Erah was here, in the same

plane of reality as Billie, the reason for Nathanial's fall.

"You remained silent when I called," he said, watching Erah's face closely.

Erah smiled. "You were worried about me?"

"Perhaps."

Erah's smile widened.

Nathanial sighed. "I thought you'd decided to shun me after all."

Erah lifted himself from the armchair—innately graceful as always—and closed the small distance between them. "I was busy."

Nathanial straighten to his feet, stare holding the other angel's, ready for the strike. His wings flared. His jaw clenched.

With another smile, Erah cupped the back of Nathanial's neck and gently pressed his forehead to his. "Ah, my brother, I really have missed you."

For a fleeting moment, Nathanial gave himself over to the intimate contact and closed his eyes. And then stepped to the side, breaking the touch.

Erah watched him, eyes flashing iridescent for a split second. "Why do you call me? Are you aching for the company of your own kind?"

For me?

The clarification whispered through Nathanial's mind, Erah's voice relaxed and confident.

They'd been so close, he and Erah. And then Nathanial had divulged everything to him about Billie and been cast out.

"Do you need my help?" Erah smiled again, returning to the armchair and dropping into it. "Your wings preened?"

Nathanial grunted. "I forgot about your woeful sense of humor. The one thing about you I do not miss."

"But you *do* miss me." Erah nodded, and once again threaded his fingers behind his head. The action stretched the white T-shirt he wore tighter over his broad chest. Emphasized the muscular frame of his torso. "I am happy now."

Crossing the living room, Nathanial closed the door leading down the hallway. If Billie was to leave her room, come looking for him, maybe the closed door would stop her. He couldn't have Erah knowing she was here.

Hiding her existence in the house from his brother was easy. A simple tweak of reality. As long as Erah didn't see her.

"A soul transaction is disrupting the Order of Actuality, Erah," he said, getting right to the point. As inconceivable as it was, now that Erah was here, Nathanial didn't like the idea of him lingering.

Why?

Why what, brother? What are you not wanting

me to know?

"Get out of my head, Erah," he instructed, turning back to the living room.

Erah grinned. "Tell me what you don't want me to know, and I will."

Nathanial rolled his eyes. "If you must... Yes, I *have* missed you. Greatly."

"Was that so hard?" *Now what are you not telling—*

"I *said*," Nathanial growled, "out of my head."

Erah raised an eyebrow, and shifted in the armchair. "Okay, okay. I forgot how often you made having fun boring. Tell me about this soul transaction. Why is it worthy of an angel's attention? Who cares what the fools do down here with their souls?"

Letting out a ragged sigh, Nathanial returned to his chair and perched on one of its arms. "This transaction is not normal. I can't find the one who orchestrated it. No demon is laying claim to it—and trust me, I have questioned the usual suspects—"

"Did you make them suffer?" Erah's eyes flashed. His perfect teeth glinted in the room's muted light. "Please tell me you made them suffer. You were so good at it, brother. You made it look like art. Watching you at work..." Erah closed his eyes and let out a satisfied groan.

"They suffered."

The screams of the demons he'd interrogated to learn what Gilbert had done with his soul still lingered in Nathanial's memories. What he'd done to those demons…

Bile bubbled up at the back of his throat.

Angels were free to deal with demons in any way they saw fit, but the way Nathanial had elicited answers in his questioning, even for a fallen angel, one not so restricted by the Laws… Well, God would have turned His back on Nathanial—if He hadn't already.

"Good." Erah nodded, pleased. "I'm glad you haven't gone soft down here. So no demon is responsible. Problematic, to be sure. And unusual. So you think it's another fallen who initiated the deal? What's the deal with the transaction, do you know? Specific details."

And here's where it gets tricky.

Telling Erah the specifics meant revealing Gilbert had sold his soul for Billie. How was Erah going to react to that?

"The soul was sold in exchange for the love of a female." How clinical and detached he sounded. "But for reasons still mysterious to me, the transaction has elevated the original owner to…something else."

Erah's eyebrows lifted. "Something else? Can you be more specific? Why do I feel like you're edging around all the information? It would be easier if you allowed me into your—"

"The thing about being a fallen, brother," Nathanial cut him off with a gentle smile on his lips, "is that you get used to not having anyone else tromping about in your head. The absence of the angel hive mind is something I've grown to appreciate."

Erah studied him, expression once again impossible to decipher. "This is a different side to you, Nathanial," he murmured. "It's…captivating."

Nathanial stayed motionless. Would Erah ignore his request to stop slipping into his mind? And if so, what would he do? He would not, could not, allow Erah in there, and not just to keep Billie's location a secret. For everything he missed about his existence before his fall, the lack of privacy from his fellow angels did not rate among them.

The autonomy of his fallen status was freeing.

"Okay." Erah rested his ankle on his bent knee and jiggled his biker-boot-shod foot. "Let's have another go at telling me what the problem is then. Use your big-boy words, brother."

A growl rumbled deep in Nathanial's chest.

Erah raised his hands. "Sorry. Sorry. Trying to lighten the mood. You're not making this easy, though."

He wasn't.

Erah had, after all, told him to come to the realm of man, fuck Billie from his system, and then forget she ever existed.

For *all* their sakes.

And in response, Nathanial had sank his sword, the weapon given to him by his Creator, deep into Erah's chest.

Their relationship had deteriorated after that.

"Brother." Erah leaned forward, resting his elbows on his knees. Behind him, the air shimmered as his wings flexed. Powerful, resplendent, white. "Whatever it is, I want to help *you*."

A gentle wave of comfort caressed Nathanial—Erah's will. Erah's soul. Reaching out to him.

You called him. He's the only one who can help. He can find Gilbert. He can find the fallen who caused this to happen.

"Let me help you," Erah said. "Please."

Without looking at the closed living room door, Nathanial felt for Billie. She was asleep.

Finally.

Deep, dreamless sleep.

Good.

Intensifying the shield concealing her from an angel's senses, he let out a breath.

"Gilbert Sanders, a man obsessed to the

point of depraved insanity with Wilhelmina Sheridan, sold his soul to make her his, but the sale has transmuted him into something darker than anything I've experienced." He stopped, swiped at his mouth, and locked his gaze on Erah. "And I can't risk tapping into his thread because his consuming lust for her feeds my own."

Chapter Five

Okay, so it was morning.

Sitting up, Billie squinted at the ridiculously cheery sun streaming through the windows.

Damn it, should have pulled the curtains before climbing into bed, eh?

Yeah, that would have been smart. Especially the ones she'd pulled all the way open in her ill-formed plan to throw herself through the window.

She tentatively rolled her shoulder, the one she knew she'd shattered in her not-so-graceful fall.

Nope. Not a single twinge of pain.

Nathanial had taken it all away.

Which *wasn't* the reason she hadn't tried to escape again. Although it did contribute. Somewhat.

The kiss...

"Jesus." Throwing off the sheet, she climbed out of bed and shuffled/lurched to the door.

There had to be a bathroom in this place somewhere, and she needed to pee. Big time.

Do angel's pee?

"Oh my God, Sheridan." She rolled her eyes and stepped out into the hallway. "Don't even go there."

The room on her left was what looked like an office. But as with the rest of Nathanial's style, it was insanely minimalistic in décor. A thriving peace lily plant filled one corner, and a large white canvas hung on the wall. The only thing on the canvas that she could see was a small smiley face emoji in the center, drawn on with what looked like black magic marker.

A glass and steel desk—complete with black leather chair—sat facing the large, curtain-free open window, beyond which was what looked like a dense redwood forest. The only things on the desk were a closed laptop and an empty wine glass.

Her lips twitched. Did he just fill up the glass with a wave of his hand when he was working? And what exactly did an angel use a laptop for?

She couldn't imagine he'd need to access Google.

Pornhub?

With another quick glance at the hand-drawn smiley face, she closed the door and moved to the room on the opposite side of the hallway.

"Wow."

It had to be his bedroom. For no other reason than it looked almost identical to the one she'd slept in with the exception of the pile of neatly stacked khaki chinos and blue jeans on the chair under the window, and a bottle of male deodorant on one of the side tables.

A giggle bubbled up through her chest. An angel using Axe. Sure. Why not?

Before she could stop herself, she stepped into the room and drew a slow breath.

His scent filled her. It was ridiculous to think she knew what he smelled like, but she did.

Even more ridiculous was how his scent made her feel. Calm. Complete.

She let out a wry grunt. If there was such a thing as Stockholm Syndrome Anonymous, when all this was over, she was joining.

Despite that, she pulled a deeper breath, eyes fluttering closed for a second, and then crossed to the bed. Running her fingers over the white linen duvet, she studied the immaculate cover, the matching pillows.

An image of Nathanial curled on his side in the middle of it, naked save for a pair of dark boxers, wings stretched out and relaxed on the mattress, filled her head.

"Definitely joining SSA when this is all over," she whispered, removing her fingertips from the bed. Did he actually require sleep?

"Well, he requires deodorant, so…"

The giggles attacked her again, snorting through her nose this time as she tried to contain them. And of course, the more she giggled, the more she needed to pee.

"Loo," she muttered. "Find it."

She hurried from the room, pausing at the threshold for one more deep breath before closing the door and crossing to the one on the right of hers.

"Ah. Found you."

She didn't waste time admiring the stunning bathroom. The toilet called.

Deed done a few moments later, she took in the room as she washed her hands. "Wow," she whispered.

A massive clawed-footed bath sat in the middle of the marble-tiled room, directly under a waterfall showerhead that looked like it belonged in a movie about billionaires. One entire wall was mirrored, and the pristine-white towels hanging on the racks looked fluffier and thicker than any she'd ever seen.

Speakers were positioned high in each corner, along with a white cylinder speaker on a shelf near the window.

Huh. A HomePod. What does an angel like to listen to while cleaning himself?

"Hey Siri," she said, eying the high-tech device. "Continue playing."

The sounds of Queen's "Bohemian Rhapsody" flooded the room.

Loudly.

"Shit!" she startled. "Hey Siri, stop! Stop!"

Silence.

Heart thumping fast in her throat, she slumped against the counter and let out a shaky laugh.

Okay, so he had good taste in music. She had to give him that.

Returning her attention to the bath, she plucked at her thumbnail. It was too easy picturing him standing in it, face lifted to the overhead shower, naked body glistening as water streamed over his muscles and—

"Oh boy." She buried her hot face in her palms. "Stop that."

In her head, she joined him in the shower. Stepped into the bath and smoothed her hands up his exquisite torso. He turned his face from the water and smiled down at her, his hands trailing a slow path down her ribs to cup her arse. Squeeze it as he drew her closer to his—

"Stop stop stop." She about-faced, flicked on the tap and splashed cold water on her hot face.

It didn't help. She imagined him stepping up behind her, hands kissing her hips, lips kissing the back of her neck.

"Oh man," she groaned, gripping the basin's edge. When her mother said giving oneself over to the angels was the best way to a fulfilled life, she bet her mum never had *this* in mind.

Opening her eyes, she glared at herself in the mirror. "Get a grip."

Her reflection glared back, and then flicked another glance at the opulent bathtub.

"Seriously," she growled. Teeth gritted, she yanked open the top drawer. Toothpaste. That's what she needed. Toothpaste. She'd rinse her mouth out and head back to her room. Maybe via Nathanial's bedroom. A blast of Axe under the arms would make do as a stop-gap until she was back home and could have a proper shower.

Or you could just ask Nathanial to join you in his—

She damn near squeezed half the tube of toothpaste she'd found in the drawer onto her finger. Damn near gouged her gums to pieces with her nail as she furiously scrubbed at her teeth.

Damn near broke her eyelids as she fixed her stare on her reflection in the mirror. She wasn't going to look at the tub again.

She wasn't.

She didn't. Just.

Teeth clean, she hurried from the room, hurried into Nathanial's, hit her armpits with an icy stream of deodorant—not Axe, as it turned out, but something called Jack Black Pit Boss that smelled divine—and ran back to the closed door of her room.

"Well, that looked like a mission."

A soft gasp burst from her at the sound of Nathanial's voice.

Gripping the doorknob like a lifeline, she turned to face him.

Holy crap, he's just as hot as you remembered.

Standing a little way down the hallway, one shoulder pressed to the wall, he smiled at her, eyes twinkling with mirth. Behind him, the door to the living room was closed. "Did you sleep well?"

She caught herself before she could run a hand through her hair. Instead, she mimicked his relaxed stance against her doorframe. "Like an abducted actress."

He laughed, the sound low and throaty. "That good, eh?"

A smile curled her lips before she could stop it.

His nostrils flared. A muscle in his jaw bunched. "If you wish to take a shower, there are clean towels in the bathroom, plus unused soap in the top drawer, along with toothpaste and, I think, a toothbrush still in its unopened packet."

Great. She couldn't tell him she didn't *want* a shower. What would she say? *Sorry, Knight. I can't have a shower because I'm pretty certain I'll have some kind of full-blown sexual experience in there if I do. Hell, just looking at it started a porn movie in my head starring you and yours truly.*

She swallowed and nodded. "Okay. Thanks."

He studied her. "I promise, I will not enter the room, Billie. You can lock the door if you choose, but you're safe with me."

Yeah, but I'm so not safe with my own freaking imagination.

"Thanks," she repeated.

His eyes connected with hers, held her gaze, driving her heart faster and harder into her throat—and then he turned away.

"Knight?"

He froze at her call. Didn't look at her. "Billie?"

The way he said her name, the strained control, the undercurrent of a longing she felt herself in her very being, played havoc with her sanity. "Have you found Gilbert yet?"

His fingers tightened into fists for a heartbeat. For just a second the air shimmered behind him. "I'm working on it," he said.

"There are unexpected complications, but I hope to have it sorted soon."

"Okay."

He reached for the door leading into the living room. "I promise, Billie, you are safe. I will not let anyone harm you."

"Okay."

His eyes met hers over his shoulder, a quick clash that sent a lick of something hot and tight into her core. "Enjoy your shower."

"Nathanial?"

"Yes?"

"I need answers. You know that, right? More than what you've given me so far."

He closed his eyes with a shaky sigh before nodding his head. "I know. And I will answer every question you ask of me."

"Okay. Thank you."

A beautiful iridescent light flared in his eyes for a second. "For abducting you?"

She smiled and rolled her eyes. "I have told you that you make a lousy comedian, haven't I?"

With a low chuckle, he opened the door, crossed the threshold and closed it behind him.

She slumped against the wall, pinching her thumbnail.

Enjoy her shower?

God help her, would she even *survive* her shower?

A dry laugh scratched at the back of her throat. Screw it. She was going to enjoy her shower, alright. Maybe if she masturbated the thought of the bastard out of her system she'd be able to get her act together. Angel or no, she was sick of the forced role of damsel in distress.

Horny damsel in distress, you mean.

"I wonder if Siri can get me the location for the nearest Stockholm Syndrome Anonymous group," she muttered, stomping back toward the bathroom.

She spent the entire time under the water doggedly thinking about anything else *but* Nathanial Knight.

Destiny's Knight's upcoming filming schedule was going to be brutal. Her character was meant to fall under the sway of a beautiful but mysterious siren of dubious motivation, leading to a love triangle between said siren, Destiny, and Destiny's true love, Benjamin Knight, a cop who also happened to be a wise-cracking werewolf with a tormented past.

Word had leaked online about the upcoming story line, and already the show was getting hate mail about the pairing. Not so much from Destamin shippers, but from Wrastiny zealots.

God, couldn't they have come up with a better shipping name for Destiny and Wraif? And really, the fact there *were* Wrastiny shippers out there still, after all the horrific, depraved things Wraif had done throughout the years, not only to Desinty, but to those Destiny loved…

"Fans are odd," she muttered, shampooing her hair.

The fans pay your mortgage.

That was true, and she loved them for it. Well, not Gilbert.

Had she ever met him? Had he ever approached her at a convention? She'd needed bodyguards at the last San Diego Comic-Con, and for a while the online gossip sites had been lathering over a supposed relationship between her and the hulking-big Scot in charge of the team. Adelaide had gleefully encouraged the rumors, feeding the ravenous horde with supposed tidbits of what Billie and Angus were up to.

More than one image of Billie and Angus eating breakfast or swimming at a private location had surfaced online, although Billie knew Adelaide was the only person who'd been aware of the moments she and Angus were together in any capacity. Every photo had been conveniently cropped to cut Riccardo—her PA—from the shot, making the situations look far more intimate than they were.

At the time, Billie had wondered if Adelaide knew of her secret relationship with the show's producer, and was using the poor Angus as a way to keep everyone's attention away from the real situation. Now, with a crazy man trying to hunt her down, she considered the very real possibility Adelaide was hoping Billie and Angus really *were* having a thing.

What better way to keep an obsessed stalker at bay than to have an intimidating Scot protecting the object of his twisted affection twenty-four seven?

Of course, Angus had quit being a bodyguard two weeks after SDCC, right around the time Billie had ended her tumultuous relationship with the show's cheating producer. She'd withdrawn from public life to lick her wounds and regroup.

And now she was being protected by an angel.

"Who is far more intimidating than Angus ever was," she murmured, reaching for the tap.

And sexier than anything else on the planet.

"And there you go thinking about Knight again."

A wave of tight heat rolled through the junction of her thighs. Her nipples beaded.

She stood still, the water rippling down her bare body, her heart racing.

For all the insanity, surreal mystery, unanswered questions and mind-bending realizations—angels? *Real* angels? Djinns? *Real* genies?—she *did* feel safe with Nathanial. She enjoyed their vocal sparring, his dry sense of humor. She appreciated his gentle calm. She couldn't help but smile anytime *he* did. As far as relationships went, it was the healthiest one she'd had since Mr. Connett, her fifth-grade teacher, who'd made everyone in his class believe they could do anything.

Was that why she'd kissed him? Because he made her feel hope? In all this craziness, she didn't only feel safe, she felt...

"Real."

The single word fell from her on a breath.

She'd spent her life pretending to be something else—the pious daughter her mother wanted, the submissive crutch her best friend wanted, the silent sexual partner her producer wanted. So many of the significant people in her life wanted her to *not* be her. Adelaide was the only one who wanted her to be herself, but even with Adelaide, Billie was something else: the actress who said the lines written for her, who turned up at the conventions and events and smiled when the cameras pointed at her.

She was none of those things with Nathanial. She felt no need to be anyone but herself with him.

And that's *why you kissed him. Because every emotion you've experienced since he entered your life has been real. Every action you've taken has been yours.*

Every action. *Every* decision. Including the decision to kiss him.

"But you can't do that again." Shaking her head, she stepped out of the bath, crossed the bathroom and slid a towel from the rack. "Because this situation *is* insane. Got it?"

Wrapping herself in the towel, she turned and looked at the bath. Pictured Nathanial standing in it…

Damn it, for her sake, she hoped the Gilbert situation was over before sundown. If she had to shower in here again, she'd masturbate herself to a puddle. Or throw herself at Nathanial and beg him to take her to sexual heaven and back.

A dry bark left her, and she turned away from the bath. "Heaven, get it? Good grief, Sheridan, you're in trouble here."

"All good?"

Closing the hallway door behind him, Nathanial slid his gaze to Erah, currently lounging in the armchair studying the tip of his left boot.

"Yes," he said, moving to the opposite armchair. "The pipes in this house are dodgy. I'll need to call a plumber. The toilet often—"

"I really don't want to know about the necessities of human bowel movements," Erah complained, raising his hands at Nathanial with an exasperated frown. "All you needed to say was this structure you now call a home makes weird noises sometimes."

"This structure I now call a home makes weird noises sometimes," Nathanial deadpanned.

Erah flashed a grin at him. "See? Was that hard?"

Thankfully, Erah had little understanding of the hows and whys of a toilet, otherwise he'd be suspicious of the fact the toilet had flushed earlier when there was meant to be no one but Nathanial in the house.

The faint sound of water running through the pipes again began to vibrate through Nathanial. The shower. Billie was in the shower.

His gut clenched. His heart quickened. What would she look like in there? If he opened the door to the room, what would she do?

Stop it.

"Have you located Gilbert?" he asked, forcing his full attention onto his brother angel.

Erah shook his head. "Unfortunately, no. You're right. There *is* something unusual about his soul transaction. I should be able to slip into his thread easily, but there's nothing."

"Dead?" A tiny shard of hope sank into

Nathanial's chest.

"No, it's as if he's concealing himself." Erah's frown grew angry. "Or perhaps it's this forsaken lump of dirt mankind walks on that's hampering my ability to detect him. You may have mastered the art of location in your fallen capacity, brother, but I wonder if I need to be...*not* here to tap into the realm?"

Nathanial dropped his head into his hands and raked them through his hair. For the last three hours, he and Erah had discussed who could possibly be responsible for elevating Gilbert from soulless, obsessed man, to what presented itself as demonic status. Erah had translocated in and out frequently, following hunches. To no avail.

At one point, Nathanial himself had risked trying to locate Gilbert's thread again, but—as Erah watched him closely, stare locked on his face, wings stretched behind him, as if ready to downward thrust—all he could sense was the weak residue of the man's depraved lust. Too faint and displaced to snag.

However, even that slight brush with Gilbert's obsessive hunger had stirred Nathanial's desire for Billie and, with a sharp hiss, he'd withdrawn his mind from the ethereal plane.

It was too dangerous.

"I'm going."

Erah's statement made Nathanial jerk his head up, and he frowned. "Going?"

Was it selfish of him to be glad? Keeping Erah unaware of Billie was exhausting.

Or is it that you just want to relax with her? Pretend you're a normal man, in the company of a woman you admire?

Perhaps, but that existence was beyond him.

Erah flashed a grin. "By the way, don't think I've forgotten you're in this mess because of the human female. Or that the very forbidden emotions you have for her have complicated things for you again. Do you want me to check in on her?"

"*No.*" Hell, he'd said that too quickly. He pulled a steadying breath. "I've got her protected. She's being watched."

Erah cocked an eyebrow.

"A djinn I know. Owes me a favor."

"You trust a djinn?" Erah shook his head. "You really have gone soft, brother. I'll be back when I find something out. Don't go anywhere."

Before Nathanial could reply, Erah vanished.

"Don't go anywhere." He slumped back in the armchair, dragging a hand down his face. "Idiot."

"You?"

Jolting straight out of the chair, he snapped

his stare on Billie, leaning against the frame of the now-open hallway door.

"Or the other guy?" she finished, a small smile playing with her lips.

"What?" He should not feel so happy to see her. Nor should he enjoy so much the act of looking at her.

She was back in his sweatpants and her black tank top. Her hair tumbled about her face in damp strands that stirred a base response in him he fought to ignore.

"You showered," he said. The soap he used lingered on her skin. He could smell it from where he stood, and that, too, stirred him.

Glibert's desire for her?

No. His own. God help him.

"I showered." Pushing herself from the doorframe, she crossed to the armchair Erah had just been sitting in and dropped into it. "So, who's the idiot? You, or the guy who just," she lifted her hands to her shoulders and flapped them three times in quick succession, "flew away?"

"Erah." He smiled. "And he would not be impressed to see you reduce his wings to such a small span."

"Ahh, so he *is* another angel?" She nodded, clearly impressed with herself. "I figured as much."

"He does radiate a certain grace."

She laughed. "It was more the arrogance and mightier-than-thou attitude I was talking about. It's a very angel thing."

"Hey."

Her eyes twinkled. "Okay, you're not as bad as you were when we first met."

Grinning, he dipped his head in a small nod. "Thank you. I'm flattered. I think."

"Welcome. Was I right in not coming out here? Waiting until he left?"

With a sigh, he lowered himself back into his chair. "You were. Erah is helping me locate Gilbert, true, but he's not—" He stopped himself from saying *your biggest fan*.

An understatement, to be sure.

Fuck her and forget her. That's what Erah had said about Billie an eternity ago—and he'd said the very same words after Nathanial had revealed who Gilbert was obsessed with.

"Fuck her, brother," Erah had snarled at him from the very chair she now sat in. *"Fuck her until you shake the very walls of Heaven. Indulge yourself in the carnal pleasures the human female offers, and then forget her. Purge her from your mind and soul, erase her from your thoughts completely so you can refocus on your true purpose, and maybe return to where you truly belong. Fuck her and forget her."*

A soft laugh fell from Billie and she repositioned herself, Buddha style, in the chair.

"He's not into humans?"

Nathanial smiled. "Let's go with that."

She laughed again. "Okay. So…do you have an update? When am I safe to be set free in the world again? True, the show is on hiatus at the moment, but my absence is going to be noted at some point. Unless you have someone pretending to be me back in LA. Please tell me you don't have someone pretending to be me back in LA."

"Worried your fans will catch on?"

She blinked. "No. God no. Have you seen the way I interact with fans? I'm pretty crazy. I don't think they ever know what to expect from me. No, I'd hate the thought someone could get hurt pretending to *be* me. As it is, I'm a little worried for the look-a-likes on Hollywood Boulevard. What if Gilbert is so far…gone, he goes after one of them thinking she's me?"

"He won't."

She frowned. "And you know this how?"

How much did he tell her? "When a human sells their soul for something or someone, they become immediately and irrevocably entwined with that thing. Or person."

Her frown deepened. "So what you're saying is, Gilbert now has this, what? Connection to me? And he knows where I am?" She pinched her thumbnail, her teeth pulling at her bottom lip. "I don't think I like that idea at all."

Nathanial sighed. "It's one of the reasons I had to remove you from your home. Distance you from anyone who could get hurt."

And the other reason?

He swallowed.

Self-contempt and guilt boiled through him at the other reason.

He wanted her to get to know him. He knew her…her heart, her soul. Her fears. He knew she questioned daily if she was worth the attention and adoration her fans gave her, knew she wondered if the people nice to her only were so because she was famous. He knew she anonymously gave almost a quarter of her income to animal shelters, not seeking recognition for it, just wanted to help neglected living creatures find love.

He knew she dialed her mother's number every night, the mother who told her she was nothing but a slut, a whore, for choosing to become an actress. He knew she sat listening to the dial tone, waiting, aching for her mother to answer the call. He knew she cried tears of pain and heartache and rejection every night when her mother didn't.

He knew her.

But she knew nothing of him.

That was the way it was meant to be, the way it *should* be.

Until he'd denied his Creator's Word and

fallen for her.

In every way an angel could.

"So what happens now? How long will it take this Error of yours—"

"Erah." He chuckled at her mispronunciation.

"How long will it take— Wait." Her frowned returned. "Why can't *you* find Gilbert?"

Tapping into Gilbert's thread ignites my own desire for you.

He opened his mouth—and closed it. He couldn't lie to her. It was impossible. An angel could not lie to a human.

"Does this have something to do with your scream last night? Did you try to find him then?" Her spine stiffened and her jaw clenched. "Did he hurt you somehow?"

The anger in her voice sent a wave of warmth through him. And a cold finger of acceptance. He was not recovering from this. Erah may believe Nathanial one day capable of returning to Heaven, but Erah was deluded.

He was not just drawn to her, attracted to her.

He loved her.

From that, there was no coming back. No reprieve.

No forgiveness.

Screwed. He was screwed.

"He didn't hurt me." It wasn't a lie, but he was skirting a fine line of truth. "But I am…" He swiped at his mouth. "I am vulnerable to what feeds him."

"What feeds… You mean his…" She licked her lips, her eyes dropping to his for a split second. "His obsession with me?"

"Yes."

"So you can't find him, because it makes you…what?"

He didn't answer. Drew a slow breath.

She studied him. "I asked you a while ago if this whole…saving me thing was a standard angel procedure, offered to any human in this kind of trouble, and you didn't really answer. I'm going to ask you again. What's the deal with you—*you*, Knight—helping me, protecting me from Gilbert? Are you doing it because it's your duty as an angel? Or…for *other* reasons?"

She had him. He could not lie. He could refuse to answer her question, but that in itself was an answer, one that would terrify her. She'd fill in the blanks herself. What would she fill those blanks with?

What kind of monster would he become?

He opened his mouth.

And closed it.

Shifting a little in the chair, she let out a choppy laugh. "Y'know what, let's start with some other questions that might be easier for you to answer. Ready?"

He narrowed his eyes. "Ready."

He wasn't. Not at all.

Another shaky laugh. "Alright. Let's start with the *really* easy ones. Are all angels like you? How many of you are down here on Earth? Is there really a God, and if so, which religion got it right?"

He blinked.

She grinned. Waited.

"Umm." How the hell did he answer? "*Those* are the easy questions?"

Rolling her eyes, she wriggled deeper into the armchair. "Okay, try these ones on for size. I know you mentioned a djinn—James the genie, right?—but what other supernatural beings are moving around with us humans?" She frowned. "Just out of interest, did you know there's a TV show called *Supernatural*? How accurate is it? And come to think of it, how accurate is *my* show?" Her frown turned playful. "*Supernatural* is on network, so we're on the opposite ends of the viewership spectrum—no real sex or tits and arse on *their* show. Plus, the main protagonists are all male, whereas I'm clearly a female." She stopped, an enigmatic glint in her eyes. "As you can see."

Hell, he could see.

Throat tight, body growing tighter, he

arched an eyebrow at her. "Which question do you want me to answer first?"

She grew still. Her heart beat faster, disrupting the air between them. Charging it with an energy he could feed off for a lifetime. "The first one."

"Are all angels like me?"

"No. Are you doing all this, protecting me, saving me, because it's your duty as an angel?" She held his gaze. Imprisoned him with hers. "Or for *other* reasons?"

"Both."

She drew a swift breath at his answer.

"I'm not..." He swiped a hand over his mouth, scrunched up his face and uttered a short laugh.

Now or never. "I'm a fallen angel, Billie. I've lost my Creator's favor. My fellow angels have shunned me—with the exception of Erah."

Eyes wide, she stared at him. "Why?"

"Because of you. I fell because of you."

"*What?*"

Her heart smashed faster in her chest. He wanted to press his palm to her breast and slow its rapid beat. He wanted to brush his thumb over her bottom lip and show her how he saw her.

He wanted to take the words back.

He wanted to tell her everything.

"Your existence, your life force, the spark

that would one day become you…called to me an eternity ago. An eon before you were even born, I was aware of you. And that awareness shifted my existence. Altered my purpose. And as a consequence, I was given two options: expunge my awareness, or be banished from the only home I'd ever known."

She stared at him.

Expunge my awareness. What a clinical, emotionless way to say *forget you*.

But when it came to Billie, his emotions ruled him. Emotions angels were never meant to have.

"You're still aware of me," she said, her voice low. "So I guess that means you…"

"I would rather be cut off from the only existence I know, the only one I knew for thousands of human years, than to deny your place in my heart."

"You fell for me," she whispered.

"I fell for you."

A complicated internal conversation took place in her mind. He watched it unfold on her face, although he had no clue what her thoughts were.

She regarded him silently, eyebrows dipped in a frown, and then released a slow breath. "Well, fuck."

He let his lips curl in a slow, wry smile. "As much as I would like to, we—"

She unfurled from her armchair, closed the small distance between them and—gaze once again holding his—slowly and purposefully straddled his hips. Her bent legs snugging close to his thighs, her sex aligning to his, her fingers combing through the hair at the back of his head.

"Billie," he groaned, her name little more than a hoarse breath. "You—"

She kissed him.

Sex to his, hands holding his head exactly where she wanted it, she swiped her tongue against his lips, demanding he open his mouth to hers.

He did. There was no point in fighting. He wanted this, wanted *her*. Had for longer than he could remember.

Her tongue found his, mated with it. Her hands balled tighter in his hair. She rolled her hips, aligning her heat closer to his.

He growled, smoothing his hands up her back as he thrust his hips. Letting her know without words he was hers.

She deepened the kiss, matching his hunger.

His head swam. The blood in his veins—the blood of the human body he'd assumed when expelled from his place of creation—turned hotter. Surged through him, elevating his heart rate.

Her taste, her smell, her fire, her force...

Everything he'd fallen in love with, being given to him by the woman he'd changed everything for...

Another giddy wave crashed over him. He drew her closer, reveling in the sensation of her back muscles beneath his palms. So warm and yielding, and at the same time so full strength. So human; fragile and yet formidable.

She shifted her mouth on his, nipping at his bottom lip, before demanding more of his mouth again.

He chuckled, a low, throaty response to her hunger, the same craving he felt for *her*, and moved his hands to her hips. Squeezing them, he pushed his groin up again, the heat at the junction of her thighs against his length— trapped by his jeans—an exquisite torment.

A carnal caress he never believed he'd ever experience.

Could this even be true? Had he been cast out so thoroughly he was really in Satan's hands, being tortured with his truest desire?

Billie's hands raked down the back of his neck, her nails scoring his flesh as she once again ground her sex to his engorged erection, detonating a raw urgency in him.

Soon. Soon...

With a groan, she tore her lips from his, her breath choppy and shallow as she stared down into his eyes. "Holy crap," she whispered, fingers feathering over his jaw, his throat, his heaving chest. "What was that?"

A cold finger sank into his heart. "I did *not* make you do that, Billie. I assure you, I promise you, I did not exert my influence over—"

She silenced him with a fierce, quick kiss, before settling back on his lap again. A smile curled her lips. "I know."

He swallowed. "You do?"

"I do."

"Why did you..." He stopped. Swallowed again. "Why did you kiss me?"

She traced his bottom lip with her thumb, her smile dancing in her eyes. "Because a person who thinks for themselves is hot. An *angel* thinking for himself? Well, that's just insane levels of hotness."

He laughed, exploring her back with his hands. "I do fear that opinion would be frowned upon where I come from."

Rolling her hips, she slipped her hands down over his chest. "I don't give a flying fuck," she said, and pulled her tank top over her head.

Nathanial froze.

Emotions rushed at him. Thoughts, fears. Surprise. Rapture.

Mouth dry, pulse pounding, he lowered his eyes, his throat growing thick at what she'd presented him. "You are beautiful. Truly beautiful."

She was.

"Flawless," he whispered, looking into her eyes again.

"I don't know what you just said," a smile played with her lips, "but it sounded pretty."

He frown, replaying the moment. "I'm sorry. I didn't realize…" He let out a wry laugh. "I was speaking Enochian."

"Angel language?"

"Angel language. Humans are not meant to be able to hear Enochian."

"I did. Have done a few times. When you said something back at my place when Rhames arrived, and now. I don't understand *what* you're saying, but I can hear it."

Another reason she was so special. She heard him speaking his natural language and survived.

"What did you say in Enochian?" she asked, studying him closely.

He smiled. "I said flawless. Because you are. Flawless."

Rolling her eyes, she grinned. "Well, in that case, you totally know how to say the right things."

He laughed.

"Now…" She reached behind her and circled his wrists with her hands. "Let's see if you know how to *do* the right—"

"Ahem." Someone cleared their throat in

the living room.

Nathanial flattened Billie to his chest. His wings wrapped around her, protecting her with a shield no human—and few nonhuman—forces could penetrate. The full strength of his power charged through him as his stare locked on the man standing behind her.

"What the hell are you doing here, James?" he ground out. A million icy-cold pin-pricks of excruciating pain traversed his skin as he released his hold on his power and allowed it to dissipate back into his body. "I almost killed you."

James cocked an eyebrow, his eyes roaming the ceiling as he rubbed at the back of his neck. "Maybe I should have knocked first?"

"You think?" Billie shot back, twisting on Nathanial's lap to glare over her shoulder at him.

James laughed, flicked her the quickest of grins, and then snapped his stare back to the ceiling at Nathanial's growl. "Not looking, not looking." He pointed his index finger upward. "You know your ceiling needs painting, right?"

"Why are you here?" Nathanial smoothed his palms up Billie's back and let his wings relax again, even as he scowled at the djinn.

"I truly hate to ruin your fun." James shuffled his feet, head tilted back farther as he continued to check out the ceiling. "But that situation I talked to you about earlier?"

A wave of cold swept through Nathanial, and he drew his arms closer around Billie. "What about it?"

James's throat worked as he lowered his head and fixed his focus on Nathanial. "It's happened again. Three times."

Stepping over the charred lump at his feet, Wraif sucked in a deep breath.

Agitation slithered through his veins, a hungry parasite demanding to be fed. Each life he burned away gave him a brief glimpse of where his Destiny was, like the blinding flash of a lightning bolt on a human retina. But each glimpse lasted fewer and fewer seconds, and the tug on his existence—the pull he *knew* was his Destiny calling out for him, begging him to find her, take her from the angel—lingered an even shorter time.

He was consuming life forces at a rapid rate, and yet he still starved for what he required.

Why?

What had been different about the cop?

He spoke Destiny's other name, the soundless voice—absent for a long time—whispered in his head. *He had a connection to her, no matter how tenuous, a link to her soul. It gave you more of what you needed...*

More. To find her, he needed to gorge on a life force closely entwined with his Destiny's.

Yes. And you know who that life belongs to. You know who will feed you until you're replete with what you need.

He did.

Smiling, he turned to the blubbering human cowering against the back wheel of the car he'd flagged down earlier, when the tug had faded to nothing.

The man he'd smiled at through the driver's window, made small talk with, chuckling about how silly he was to have run out of gas and asking if the guy could help him out, as he was on his way to see his girl and didn't want to be late.

The man who said he'd love to help, sure, no problems at all. Was he okay with making a quick side trip so he could drop his "old man" off at the track?

Later, the man had begged Wraif not to hurt him, to take his father instead, oh God, please take "the old fuck," not him, when Wraif had opened his door and pulled him from behind the wheel. Had gibbered and sobbed on the ground as Wraif had dragged the elderly man from the passenger seat and unleashed the burn, incinerating him, feeding off him…

Hurry, the invisible voice urged. *The angel is going to have her soon.*

Hate blasted through Wraif, and he smiled at the pathetic human male on the ground. "You can drive me to where I need to go," he said. "Or you can die the same way your father did. You decide."

Chapter Six

So this was a genie. Or rather, a djinn.

Billie tucked her knees closer to her chest, studying the tall, rangy man with the shaggy light brown hair, hawkish nose and *Yoda for President* T-shirt talking to Nathanial.

He didn't look like one. His ear wasn't even pierced.

She bit her bottom lip to stop herself from chuckling. Talk about being a victim of the Hollywood education program. Earring. *Pft.* More to the point, why wasn't he blue? And bald?

She bit her lip again and hid her mouth behind her knees.

Whatever the reason for the djinn to miraculously appear in Nathanial's living room, interrupting the best kiss she'd ever been a part of and preventing what would've been—no doubt at all—the best foreplay she'd ever experience, it probably was a dire one. Giggling was most likely highly inappropriate right now.

Would help if they told me what was going on, instead of standing over in the kitchen muttering to each other.

James had materialized a few minutes ago. In that time, she'd put her tank top back on—handed to her by the djinn as he kept his stare on the ceiling—climbed off Nathanial, and settled back into the armchair as he and James strode into the kitchen, voices low. They'd stayed that way, flicking her the occasional quick glance.

Screw this.

"Hey!"

Both Nathanial and James jumped at her shout. The air behind Nathanial shimmered as his stare locked on her.

She scowled at them, butting her chin on her knees. "Any chance either of you are going to fill me in at some point soon on the reason for James the Genie's appearance here?"

James chuckled and gave Nathanial a smirk. "Well, she's not a wilting damsel in distress, that's for certain."

"See?" Billie waved her hand at James in a there-you-go gesture, as she fixed Nathanial with a pointed look. "*See?*"

He answered with a drawn-out sigh.

James chuckled again. "Dare I say you're like an old married couple?"

"Watch it with the *old* comment, James." Billie directed a mock glower his way. "I can't speak for Knight, but twenty-six is far from old."

James bowed with a flourish of his hand. "Apologies, fair maiden."

"Oh no, don't call me that, either. Billie will do."

He smiled. "Billie it is." He arched a look at Nathanial, standing beside him with his arms crossed and an unreadable expression on his face. "I like her."

Again, the air behind Nathanial shimmered into the shape of large wings for a split second. Whatever he did to keep them concealed, it was clearly having a hard time today.

James laughed. "Reel in the jealousy there, Feathers—"

"Feathers?" Billie raised her eyebrows.

"I'd rather you not call me that," Nathanial said, sliding a look her way.

"I'd rather not be kept in the dark about what's going on," she shot back, "but hey, I'm currently sitting alone in a chair that a few moments ago was the location for some pretty amazing making out, while you two mutter over there, so…" She shrugged, holding Nathanial's gaze.

He let out a slow breath and clawed a hand through his hair. "You are going to be the end of me, Wilhelmina Sheridan."

"I'd rather that not be the case," she answered, heart thumping fast. "Feathers."

He blurred into an indistinct fracture of iridescent light—and suddenly stood directly in front of her.

She gasped. And then moaned, happiness flooding her as he framed her face in his palms and brushed his lips over hers.

"Argh. Get a room, you two."

"We did," Nathanial threw over his shoulder. "And you materialized *into* it."

Billie smiled.

Nathanial traced his thumb over her lip and then straightened, turning back to James.

For a fleeting second, the softest of invisible caresses kissed Billie's face. An unseen touch of something soft and delicate.

His wings?

Her heart soared. Her soul did the same. She closed her eyes, at once calm and serene yet aching for more…

And then, like a wave ebbing away from the sand, the sensation faded, leaving a sense of contentment and hope.

Opening her eyes, she frowned up at Nathanial's back. With one touch, he could make her the horniest person on the planet, and with another the most at peace. How did she align the two responses?

She tugged at her thumbnail, watching him move back to where James leaned against the kitchen counter.

Was it possible to be in love with someone so quickly? Or was she truly going in—

"Hey?" she burst out, scrambling to her feet. "You still haven't told me what's going on."

James snorted.

Nathanial's shoulders slumped. "Damn it," he muttered.

She glared at him. "So the kiss just now, the stroking from the wings, that was just to try to sidetrack me?"

"Wings?" He spun back to her, his gaze finding hers. "What do you mean, the *stroking from the wings*?"

"Just now, when you turned back to genie-boy over there. I felt something soft, like feathers, brush against my face."

"That's not possible. My wings exists in a different realm when I'm concealing them from humans. They have no substance in this realm. They can't be felt by anyone."

Heart smashing fast in her chest, she deepened her glare at him. "Well, as you keep pointing out, I'm not just anyone, 'cause I felt them."

"Is this a lovers' spat?" James called from the

kitchen. "I'm feeling like this is a lovers' spat. Do you want me to leave?"

"No," Billie growled.

"No," Nathanial ground out.

"Okay, okay." James raised his hands.

"I want answers," Billie said, stomping toward Nathanial. "*All* the answers. I want to know why I can feel your wings when apparently I'm not meant to, why I can hear you speak Enochian when I shouldn't be able to, but more importantly right now, I want to know what's going on. What's 'happened again'? Three times? What's the 'situation' you two talked about earlier?"

"Billie," Nathanial said. "I don't want you to be upset by what Gilbert—"

"I'm way past upset on that front, Nathanial. And I'm only going to get worse with you treating me like a delicate little flower that can't handle the shit going down."

A muscle ticked in his jaw.

James cleared his throat. "Not to tell you how to angel, Nath, but she's got a point. I don't know what's going on between you two, obviously something fairly intense—I'm getting the feeling Billie here is in some way related to your fall from High—but keeping her in the dark about the threat somehow connected to her?" He shook his head at Nathanial. "That's not right. Or smart. And this is coming from *me.*"

"Listen to the genie." Billie pulled an apologetic face. "I mean James."

Nathanial studied her, expression closed, and then swung back to James. "I'm going to make your life a living hell after this, you know that, right?"

James grinned. "Yep."

"Just so you know. And are prepared." With a ragged sigh, Nathanial turned back to Billie. "Remember when I told you the sale of Gilbert's soul was unlike any I'd seen before?"

She straightened her spine and gave him an impatient expression. Better to show him she wasn't freaking out than to admit she *was* freaking out. Just when she thought she'd gotten her head around this unexpected insight into a whole other world she'd previously believed fictional, her angel protector/abductor goes and pulls the serious card and her heart turns into a sledgehammer.

"Yes," she said. Damn it, her voice was croaky again. And why the hell was her heart trying to thump its way out of her chest?

Nathanial rubbed at the back of his neck, searching her eyes.

"Just tell me," she whispered. "Please? I think you owe me that, given I've been a pretty good abductee."

A small smile curled at the edge of his

mouth and he dropped his hand with another sigh. "Given how completely I've upturned your life, you have been...amazing."

The compliment sent a little lick of surreal delight through her. After all this, she'd need a shrink. "Thank you. Now, tell me."

Behind him, James levered himself from the counter and made his way into the living room to perch on the edge of the coffee table next to where they stood.

Nathanial nodded, wiped at his mouth, and then fixed her with a direct, unwavering look. "Somehow, the sale of Gilbert's soul transformed him into something no longer human."

Billie swallowed. An icy clamminess slithered over her body. No longer human. Oh yay. "What does that mean, exactly?"

The muscle in Nathanial's jaw bunched again. "I think he's transmutated into something possibly demonic—or worse."

"There's something worse than demonic?"

His nostril flared as he dipped his head. "And I believe him to be more dangerous than I first thought."

Damn it, where had all the warmth gone in the room? "In what way? I'm alright here, aren't I? Safe?"

"Yes. You are. But earlier, while you were sleeping, James projected himself here to tell me about—" He stopped, swiping at his mouth again.

"Do you want me to tell her?" James asked.

"No, no." Nathanial shook his head, gaze holding Billie's. "This is something I must do."

Chest tightening, she frowned. Waited. Even as a part of her wanted to run to her room and lock the door.

"I think Gilbert is burning people alive. But not naturally."

A sickening ball of ice rolled in her gut. "There's a natural way to burn people alive?"

Oh God, what kind of nightmare had she been thrust into?

Nathanial's Adam's apple slid up and down his throat.

She hugged herself. "How do you...why do you know this?"

"We have a wiccan at Guarded Souls who can detect when dark magic or power is being used. When that happens, we investigate. While we're just a standard protection agency to the outside world, we do tend to constantly monitor the...existences we come from. When the malevolent force of the first incineration triggered Nim's internal radar, two of our team checked it out."

"Okay." Her mouth tasted like old dust. "So why does this have anything to do with me? With Gilbert? Wait..." She stared at

Nathanial. "Who did Gilbert kill?"

Please don't say Adelaide. Or Riccardo. Or—

"Detective Rhames," Nathanial answered. "The cop whose will I," he flicked James a quick look, "influenced outside your home."

Oh no.

"The big nice guy who tried to save me from you?"

"Yes."

"He's dead now? Because of me?"

"No. Not because of—"

"Did Gilbert kill the cop who was sent to protect me, Nathanial?" The ice in her veins cracked. Anger rushed through her. "Did he somehow burn him alive? Using some kind of dark...magic he got *only* because he sold his soul to have me?"

"Billie!"

She shook her head and took a step back. "So the nice cop who was only doing his job is dead because of me. Burned to death because of me." She balled her fists, gritting her teeth. God, if she threw up now...

"If it helps," Nathanial said softly, "his soul was pure. He will be going to—"

"No, it doesn't fucking help!"

"I'm sorry."

Grief and rage warred within her. At the pain in her heart for Detective Rhames, at the sorrow and failure in Nathanial's eyes, at the hate overwhelming her for Gilbert.

But mostly, at the sense of being useless now.

She dropped into the armchair, chest tight. An image of Rhames filled her head, taunted her.

"Billie—" Nathanial said again.

She snapped her glare up to him, and then locked it on James. "You said it's happened again. Three times."

James gave Nathanial a quick glance, and then nodded. "Yes."

"Do you know who the…the people are? Who he killed?"

"No."

"Why is he doing it?"

Another quick look at Nathanial. Was he scared to reveal too much? Worried for her sanity? Or his safety? "It looks like he's feeding on their life force," he said. "That's what Nim is thinking."

"Excellent." The word tore from her, acrid with sarcasm and contempt. "He couldn't just go through a McDonald's drive-thru?"

Neither Nathanial nor James laughed. She would have hit them if they had.

"Do you know why he killed them, in particular?"

James shook his head. "The first two victims after the cop outside your place were a few miles apart heading east. I made the assumption he somehow knew where you and Feathers were and was heading this way. But the third was farther west again. Just outside San Merino."

San M—

"No!" She jolted to her feet. "Adelaide!"

"What?" James frowned.

Oh no. No! San Merino…

"Nathanial." She swung to him. "Adelaide lives in San Merino."

He jabbed a finger at James. "Don't leave her alone."

"Wh—"

His form shattered into a prism of shimmering light, and he vanished.

"Fuck!" James yelped, almost scurrying backward across the coffee table. "I've never seen the winged bastard do— Hey, where are *you* going?"

Sprinting for the door, any door, she didn't slow down at James's stunned shout. She had to get to Adelaide.

"Stop." James materialized directly in front of her, hands out.

She careened into him, stumbled sideways, and started running again.

"Billie," he called. "Stop."

Where the hell was the front door? Where the fuck was the—ahh, there.

She bolted for what looked like the front entry-way foyer.

And stumbled to a halt as James once again appeared in front of her.

"I need to get to Adelaide!"

"And you're what? Going to run to her?"

"I need to…to…" Frustration and worry ate at her.

He nodded, palms out to her. "I get it. I truly do. I have no idea who this Adelaide is you need to get to, but if Gilbert—or whatever Gilbert is now—is after you, going to where he'll be is *not* a good idea. Besides, Feathers will protect her."

"*If* she's still alive." Sucking in a choppy breath, she stared at him. Maybe if she rammed her shoulder into his—

"The last victim was male," he said. "And no, I'd rather you *didn't* try to shoulder-barge me into the wall."

She blinked. "How did you know I was thinking of doing that?"

"I'm very good at reading people. It's a djinn thing." He preened a little. "Hey, apparently I'm also good at being a poet…without knowing—"

"Don't say it," she warned.

"It," he finished. His smile grew gentle. He didn't, however, drop his hands.

She let out a sigh and slumped against the

wall. "Do you really think Nathanial will be able to keep Adelaide safe?"

"I do. I don't know how much *you* know about him, but Feathers is one of the most formidable bastards I've ever known. And I'm over five thousand years old."

Her mouth fell open. She snapped it shut, wincing when her teeth click together. "Until twenty-four hours ago, the only...paranormally, nonhumany stuff I had any knowledge of was what the writers wrote for my show. Now..." She shook her head.

James leaned his shoulder against the wall, his eyes as kind as his smile. "If it's any consolation, most of us who don't fall into the human category are pretty alright. And we spend a lot of our time making sure the malevolent evil pricks among us are kept in check. Nathanial? He's one of the best."

She swallowed and nodded. "I know. It's stupid, but in my heart, my soul, I know. It's just..."

"This is all still a huge shock to the system?"

"Huge." She rubbed her face and pushed herself from the wall. "So, what do we do now? Wait? Worry? Pace the floors?"

"We could do that." James also straightened from the wall. "Or we could eat breakfast? I've been working all night and I'm starving. What do you think?"

Her stomach grumbled. Loud enough that James laughed.

She rolled her eyes. "Okay, so apparently breakfast is a good idea. Although I have no idea if Nathanial has any food here. To be honest, I don't know if angels eat."

"Oh, angels eat. They don't have to, but they do. At least, Feathers does. I've seen him demolish an upsized XXXL Fatburger meal—with added egg, bacon and chili—in three bites and complain it wasn't enough." He grinned. "Trust me, never let him take you to a Fatburger."

Billie laughed, an image of walking with Nathanial into the Fatburger on 3rd and La Cienega Boulevard filling her head. His wings on full display, impressive and blindingly white, and everyone in the fast-food joint fainting at the magnificent sight.

A ribbon of warmth and delight unfurled through her at the thought, and she let out another soft chuckle.

Who would have thought she could laugh, find happiness, with everything going on?

"So, what do we do," she asked, walking toward the kitchen, "if there's no food here? I have no idea where we actually are, nor do I know if there's a car we could go in. I'm going to assume you didn't drive here, what with the way you suddenly appeared in the—"

She stumbled to a halt as James held up a large bottle of OJ and a carton of eggs.

He grinned. "Djinn. I'm awesome at getting stuff when it's needed. And even better at granting wishes…when the mood takes me."

She gaped at the breakfast staples in his hands. "Um, any chance I could have…I don't know, a pair of jeans and a T-shirt?"

"Did you rub my lamp?"

She blinked.

"Kidding. I don't have a lamp." He winked, and continued walking toward the kitchen, swinging the bottle of juice as he went. "But after breakfast, I'll see what I can—"

The air splintered into a million pinpricks of iridescent light directly in front of them, and Nathanial appeared.

"Miss me?"

"Are you *sure* she's safe?"

Returning his glass to the table, Nathanial fixed Billie with a steady gaze. "I'm sure she's safe. She's currently in the presidential suite at the Beverly Wilshire, enjoying an all-day, in-room spa indulgence. I've warded the suite and have dampened her soul's footprint on the Order of Actuality."

"The Order of what?"

"Actuality. The grand pattern, the scheme of all existence. I've made sure Adelaide's presence in the Order of Actuality is shuttered so if anyone tries to locate her on the temporal or ethereal plane via nonhuman means, I'll know. And then Kade will deal with them."

"You don't want Kade on your ass," James said, placing a plate piled high with scrambled eggs and bacon in front of Nathanial before slipping into the seat next to him. "That vamp is a scary bastard."

Nathanial dropped his attention to the food. With the energy he'd needed to implement the various shielding wards on Adelaide Williams, her hotel room, *and* Billie's PA, Riccardo Zaicos—whose free will was the easiest to influence Nathanial had ever encountered—he should be ravenous for any form of nutrient, even non-spiritual sustenance.

But he couldn't bring himself to pick up his fork, despite how good a cook James was (*surprisingly* good, for a being who could conjure up whatever he wanted to eat with a click of his fingers).

The vile wisps of Gilbert's corruption he'd tasted upon materializing in Adelaide's home still sickened him. Gilbert had been close. Close enough for Nathanial to consider waiting for his arrival.

The thought however, of what it would do to Billie if somehow Gilbert overpowered him and Adelaide was hurt or killed changed his mind.

He'd warded Adelaide and got her out of there with two words. Deposited her in the hotel suite, warded it, and then influenced the staff at the desk to make sure she wasn't allowed to leave the hotel until instructed by him to do so.

Racing against time, he'd returned to her house, ready to tear Gilbert asunder.

But Gilbert's taint had faded.

Desperate, he'd searched for fresh wisps of the man, knowing the effect it would have on his desire for Billie.

He'd found one tenuous, fragile thread, and snagged it.

And released it instantly, Gilbert's dark lust and ravenous obsession almost devouring him through the minute connection.

Worried, he'd translocated to the only other person Billie truly cared about in the US, Riccardo, hoping to detect the unhinged stalker there. He hadn't. Knowing the young man could still be a target, he'd slipped his influence into the free will of Billie's PA and did what he had to do to keep him safe.

Riccardo was now on his way to visit his mother in Canada. A long road trip, to be sure, but one that removed the possible threat to his life.

Nathanial had considered the notion of

using him as bait, but to do so would destroy any trust Billie had in him.

Instead, he'd cast a shielding ward around him as well, and returned to his home in the Angeles National Forest.

And the moment he'd seen Billie, Gilbert's lust had roared.

"Feathers?"

He jerked his stare up from his plate and frowned at James. "Sorry. What did you say?"

James arched an eyebrow. "I said, maybe we should introduce Bill here to Kade?"

Bill.

Hot jealousy flare at the friendly nickname. Cold rage surged through him. Not *his* rage, not *his* jealousy—Gilbert's.

Control it. Expel it. Exorcize it. Now.

Grinding his teeth, he forced the unhinged need from his soul.

"Nathanial?"

He turned to Billie, drawing warm comfort from her voice. He smiled at her—*his* smile, not Gilbert's. "I'm okay."

He wasn't. And he wouldn't be until Gilbert was dealt with.

She narrowed her eyes at him. "Yeah, I'm not buying it."

He smiled again. She gave him strength. How was that possible? The only strength an angel could draw on was that of his fellow angels and his Creator.

She felt your wings. That's not possible, either.

It wasn't, and yet she had.

"So what happens now?" She picked up her fork and scooped up some eggs. "Adelaide is safe, but Gilbert is still out there? Will he keep...burning people, feeding from them, until he finds me?"

He didn't answer. She would not like the only one he could give her.

She frowned at him, then at her eggs. "Why don't we use me as bait, then?"

"No."

Her frown deepened at his flat rebuke. "You'd rather innocent people die? What kind of angel are you?"

"The kind that knows what's in store for you if Gilbert achieves his goal."

A hot glint flared in her eyes. "If that's meant to scare me, you don't know me the way you keep saying you do."

"Time out," James said. "Time out."

Nathanial glared at him. "Now's not the time for your flippancy, djinn."

"Probably not, angel." James inched his chair back and clunked his heel onto the table's edge, crossing his other ankle over it. "But it's time for some hard truth, genie style." He pointed his index finger at Billie. "For both of you."

"James," Nathanial growled. He wasn't in the mood for this. He needed Billie to understand the danger she was in. Use her as bait? Was she insane?

Threading his fingers behind his head, James didn't flinch from his hard stare. "When Nim detected the dark power of Gilbert's first attack, she tried to find the source. It's ancient. Older than any she's experienced. Maybe even older than you, Feathers. By the third attack, she was scared."

Nathanial sucked in a quiet breath. In the years he'd known Nimue Brynn, the wiccan had never once been scared.

James turned his unwavering gaze to Billie. "So the idea of using *you* as bait? When we're dealing with a dark magic of this power? Yeah, I'm with Feathers."

"Thank you."

James raised his eyebrows at Nathanial. "I'm not finished. You have to stop being so stubborn about this whole lone-avenger deal you've got going on and ask for help. You've got friends with some serious nonhuman clout, mate. Tap that. Use it. Let us help you."

Nathanial shook his head. "It's too—"

"If you say 'dangerous,'" James said, "you'll find yourself suddenly stuck in a broken elevator covered in trapping wards in Siberia." He grinned. "You know I can do it. With just a click of my fingers."

He could. Nathanial had once seen him translocate Kade to a coffin buried in the middle of a garlic field in Brussels during an argument over the microwave in the Guarded Souls' office kitchen. How or why James had an elevator designed to imprison angels in Siberia was a conversation for another time.

"You want me to ask you for help," Nathanial stated. Billie's hot stare drilled into his profile.

James nodded. "I do. *We* do. It's not that hard. Just say, 'Jimmy, old boy, can you locate this bastard Gilbert for me?'"

Could they? Could *he*? With the way Gilbert's lust infected him, debilitated him with the barest of connections, he couldn't use his own power, and Erah was… Well, Erah was being Erah.

Erah told you to forget Billie exists so you can return to Heaven. Would he really be in any rush to help?

Perhaps not, but Erah was still an angel. And no matter his opinion of mankind, an angel's purpose was to defend the good and innocent and fight malevolence and evil.

"C'mon, Nath," James said, watching him. "Three little words: Please. Help. Me."

A ragged sigh tore from Nathanial. He flicked Billie a quick glance. Agitation radiated from her, but there was no contempt in her eyes.

He sighed again. "James," he said. "Please help—"

James dropped his feet to the floor.

"—me."

A grin split James's face. He leapt up from his seat, grabbed both sides of Nathanial's head and smacked a loud kiss on his lips. "Done."

And with that, he disappeared.

The air particles convulsed, reality folded in on itself in a frenzied paroxysm only Nathanial could detect, ruffling his feathers, and then everything grew still once more.

"So what happens next?"

Anger threaded through Billie's question.

Stealing himself against her irritation, he shifted in his chair and looked at her. "I cannot use you as bait, Billie. You must understand."

Thunder flicked over her face for a heartbeat before she slumped in the chair. "You know, when I went to bed last night, I didn't expect to be having an argument with an angel and getting a lecture from a genie when I woke up. If I did, I would have, I don't know…braided my hair or something…"

A wry smile curled her lips and, pushing aside the remains of her breakfast, she folded her arms on the table and rested her cheek on them.

Her eyes found his, direct and unwavering.

"I promise you, Gilbert will pay for what he has done."

She regarded him. "I know." Her arms muffled her voice, but the anguish in it tore at him. "But I still feel useless. I feel like we should call the cops or something, and then I remember what he did to Detective Rhames, and my stomach rolls and my heart tries to bash its way out of my body and I feel even more useless and guilty and—"

He stood from his chair and rounded the table to where she sat. She watched him, expression unreadable, and only changed her position when he stopped at her side and held out his palm to her.

"What?" she asked, frowning at his hand.

"I need you to truly understand something."

Was he really going to do this?

Her frown deepened as she took his hand.

Warmth flooded through him. Warmth, hope, life… He closed his fingers around hers and held her gaze. "I need you to understand what's driving Gilbert right now."

"I know what's driving him. He wants to get into my pants, the sick prick."

He shook his head. "If only it was that…" He didn't want to say "simple." It wasn't the correct word.

Don't do this. She may never forgive you.

He swallowed. He didn't need her forgiveness. He needed her to understand.

"Ready?" he asked, searching her eyes. Could anyone ever be ready for what he was about to do?

She tilted her chin. "Sure. Hit me with it. Say it."

"Not say." He shook his head and lowered into a crouch beside. "Show."

With a slow breath, he reached into the ethereal plane, sought out Gilbert, and brushed against the thinnest, weakest of the man's wisps.

—myDestinyfuckheruntilwediolovehermine ownherfuckhermineto—

He severed his connection to the thread, immediately purging its impact on him even as he stared at Billie.

"Oh God!" Horror leeched into her face. Her eyes grew wide. Less than .25 seconds of Gilbert's obsession was enough—maybe even too much—to experience.

He let go of her hand, broke his connection with her mind, and cupped her face in his palms. "Do you understand now?" he whispered.

She stared at him, mouth open, and crumpled from the chair. Knees clunking on the floor, she buried her face into his chest.

Wrapping his arms around her, Nathanial

closed his eyes. "I'm sorry."

She clung harder to him. Her trembles quaked into his own body. His shirt grew hot, wet from her tears.

He scrunched his eyes closed and pulled her closer, resting his lips on the top of her head. He could ease her grief and fear. With a simple thought, a tendril of influence, he could remove her pain.

And in doing so, you would take away her trust in you. The one thing she aches for more than anything in her life is truth. In a life based on make-believe, she respects truth—trust—above all else.

He couldn't do that to her. As much as the thought of her in anguish tore him apart, he couldn't take away that which she valued so much: truth. *Her* truth. *Her* reality.

"I'm sorry," he whispered against her hair again.

A choked sound—part sob, part sigh—came from his chest. "Me too."

He pulled away, enough to lift her chin. Her eyes shone, but she met his gaze. "No. You don't have anything to be sorry for. You did *not* ask Gilbert for his obsession. You did *not* ask him to do this abhorrent, unnatural thing."

"I *did* force you to show me what you've been trying to protect me from."

Giving her a small smile, he brushed his

thumb over her bottom lip. "You *are* very forceful."

She snorted, rolling her eyes. "Damn right I am," she mumbled, before burrowing back into his chest. "If it's okay with you, I'm just going to stay here for a while."

"It's more than okay." He returned his lips to the top of her head. Wished her pain would go away, even as he felt it gnawing at her.

The second she fell asleep—barely ten minutes later—he scooped her up and carried her to her room. Opened the door with his mind and stepped forward.

"Your room."

He stopped at her low, almost inaudible murmur.

She shifting in his arms, eyes still closed, and slid her arm up around his neck. "I want your smell around me."

Sleep turned the words to a drowsy slur, and yet, they stoked in him a fire beyond his comprehension.

Heart pounding, he moved away from the door of the room and carried her to his.

Angels didn't require sleep, but he enjoyed the comfort the king-size bed afforded when he rested.

Crossing the room, he kept his pace slow. Moderated. She was asleep in his arms again, her breathing regular, her pulse the same.

With more care than he'd ever exerted before, he placed her on his bed.

Immediately, she rolled onto her side, snuggling into his pillow.

He smiled. Was this what human love felt like? This overwhelming, all-encompassing confusion of emotions? Powering his every thought, his every breath?

No wonder they craved it. But how did they govern it? Navigate it?

How did they *survive* it?

Erah warned she would be your undoing.

He turned to leave—and stopped when warm fingers slipped around his.

"Stay with me," Billie whispered, looking up at him. "Please."

A thick pressure wrapped around his chest.

Her eyes held his for a heartbeat before closing again. The faintest of pressure on his fingers, the briefest of tugs, told him exactly what she wanted him to do.

Rounding to the other side, he joined her on the bed, stretching out straight on his back beside her.

And bit back a groan as she rolled close and burrowed into his side.

Erah was right. She would forever be his undoing, but with just three words—*stay with me*—he willingly accepted his fate.

Until she told him to go away, he was hers.

Chapter Seven

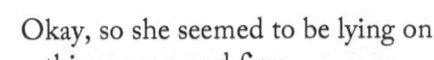

Okay, so she seemed to be lying on something warm and firm.

A sculpted chest pressed against her cheek, her left breast. Or rather, her cheek and left breast pressed against a divinely sculpted chest and torso.

Oh boy, was that an arm curled around her back? And were her thigh draped over legs? Yep, hard, corded, muscular legs.

Throat tight, pulse kicking up more than a notch, Billie opened her eyes.

So it seems I can check sleeping with an angel off my bucket list.

Not that she'd had it on her bucket list, but if she had...

He'd stayed with her.

Warmth bloomed in the pit of her belly, and

she smiled. She remembered asking Nathanial not to leave, although the fog of sleep clouded the memory now. She'd been scared the brief glimpse into Gilbert's mind would give her nightmares, but she knew if Nathanial was with her, she'd be safe.

She remembered catching his fingers with hers, asking him not to go.

She had no memory of him actually climbing into the bed with her.

But he had, he must have, because he was here now, and her dreams had been peaceful and serene.

Dreams of walking along a beautiful beach, an infinitely blue and cloudless sky sweeping overhead, the waves lapping at her bare ankles.

Dreams of Nathanial holding her hand as they soared together above the waves, the wind gentle in her hair, the brush of feathers soft on her face.

She liked those dreams.

Not wanting to disturb him—was he asleep?—she shifted her weight just enough to study his face, bringing her hand up to rest over his heart.

The steady thump beneath her palm fascinated her, as did the serenity radiating from him. It was as if a storm had passed and, in its thunderous wake, life took a deep, stilling breath.

Okay, so that was the wankiest thing you've ever thought.

Maybe. She was an actress, not a poet or a writer. And yet, the desire to define him, describe him, niggled at her.

To understand him, even as she reveled in just being with him.

She ran her gaze over his dark eyebrows, his straight nose. It was almost too big for his face, and yet it was perfect. As was the exquisite shape of his lips and the squareness of his jaw.

The urge to brush her fingertips over his stubble battled with the desire to keep feeling his heart beating beneath her palm.

Go one better…feel the warm skin of his chest with your hand.

A tight thrill shot through her, and she dropped her attention to the neckline of his shirt. Waking up beside Nathanial was incredible. Waking up beside him while they were both naked? How perfect would that be?

Biting back a groan, the junction of her thighs growing warm, she returned her attention to his face.

And found him watching her.

"Good…whatever time it is," she murmured.

He smiled, smoothing his hand along her back. "Good—"

She swiftly climbed on top of him and

kissed him silent.

A deep groan vibrated through his body, stirring something primal in her. She worshipped his mouth, his lips, his tongue, as she rolled her hips, grinding her sex to his. The rigid state of his length detonated fresh need in her, and Billie slipped her fingers beneath his shirt.

Skin on skin. Flesh on flesh.

A jolt of pure energy sank into her core, liquid electricity and concentrated life. Oh God...

He groaned again and smoothed his hands down her back to cup her arse cheeks, squeezing them.

Not enough. More.

Dragging her lips from his, she straightened, grabbed the hem of her tank top and pulled it over her head. "Make love to me," she said, throwing her shirt aside.

His nostrils flared. His palms traveled over her waist, her ribs.

She smiled. "We got interrupted last time."

"We did."

"Any way you can make sure James doesn't come back?"

He closed his eyes for a second, eyebrows dipping. The air shimmered around him, around *them*, and then he met her gaze again. "Done."

"What did you do?"

"A barrier of sorts. If anyone comes into this room, they won't be able to see or hear us."

"So we can be as loud as we like?" She wriggled her hips a little, trying not to gasp at the solid ridge pressing against her.

"As loud as we—"

She kissed him again. Hungrier this time. Holding nothing back.

Took utter control of the situation.

He moaned into her mouth, his hands exploring every inch of her body she'd bared to him.

Every. Inch.

And when that, too, wasn't enough, she broke the kiss again and moved his mouth to her breasts, first one and then the other.

He took what she gave him, his lips and tongue doing things to her no sexual partner had ever done. With every swipe and suck on her nipples, it was as if the blood in her veins was being replaced with molten pleasure. With every nip of his teeth, every molecule in her body thrummed until she balanced on an exquisite precipice.

Ribbons of delicious tension unfurled through her, from every place on her body he touched, kissed, sucked, nipped. She moaned, breaths shallow, eyes closed, and surrendering to it.

"Nathanial," she whispered, grinding harder against him as she fisted one hand in his hair and held his head exactly where she wanted it to be. "Nathanial…"

Removing his lips from the adoration of her body, he looked up at her.

"The way you say my name…" His fingers journeyed her rib cage before brushing over the puckered tip of her breast. "I wish I could explain how it makes me…"

"Makes you what?" Her skin tingled, every nerve ending attuned to him. "Feel?"

He shook his head and moved his hand up to the line of her jaw, brushing his knuckles along it. "*Everything.* The concept of speech, of names, is ancient, timeless, and we angels know the potent importance of a name more than any others. Angels have been vocalizing before the very first cell divided—but when *you* say my name, Billie, it is like everything I am, everything I have been and *will* be, becomes solid. Real."

A soft breath escaped her. Her throat thickened.

He dropped his attention to his hand, watching his knuckles feather over her jaw once more. "Angels are luminous beings, ethereal creatures of intent and purpose. The need for form, for substance, is not paramount to us. The need to exist for our purpose, that's what drives us. Compels us. And yet, when you say my name…" His Adam's apple slid up and down his throat as he returned his gaze to hers.

"Nathanial," she breathed.

Iridescent light glowed in his eyes for a heartbeat, and then—his movements slow and purposeful—he pressed her flat to her back.

His lips found hers. His tongue did the same.

He didn't rush, or demand, or control. He worshipped her lips until she feared she would melt into a puddle of euphoric pleasure, and then, as if aware she once again balanced on the brink, moved his lips to the curve of her neck, her collarbone, her shoulder.

She arched beneath him and moaned, raking her nails across his back.

He groaned—the sound raw and throaty. Unlike any sound she'd heard him make so far.

Wings. Did you touch…

The nebulous thought caressed her mind, and she smoothed her palms over his back again, near his spine, between his shoulder blades.

"Billie," he rasped, lifting his head to find her gaze. "Do you know what you're doing?"

"I didn't," she said, "until you made that sound."

Blue light flared in his eyes again before he closed them. "No human should be able to feel my wings unless I choose to let them do so, and yet you can." He opened his eyes, wonderment filling them. "Nor should I ever be able to feel a human touching them without allowing it to be so, and yet with you, I can."

She let a mischievous grin play with her lips. "You see? I *am* that special."

He laughed. "You have no idea."

He kissed her again. And then slowly removed the rest of her clothes and kissed every inch of flesh he revealed. Lingered in places Billie had once believed an angel would never linger.

Brought her to climax after climax in ways she'd once thought angels should never know.

And then, already so sated that coherent thought began to slip away, she begged him to come inside her.

He rose from the bed, removed his own clothes, and—with the tenderest, slowest thrust—Nathanial entered her.

Filled her.

Completed her.

Noooooooo!!

Wraif crumpled to the floor, the scream in his mind as deafening as the scream tearing from his throat.

The angel! The angel had...had—

He threw back his head and screamed again.

The angel had defiled her! Had pumped his sordid flesh into her body!

"*No!*" he roared.

Abhorrent impressions lashed at him, vile caresses he knew were those of the angel touching his Destiny.

He shrieked once more, blasting the burn outward, shattering the windows of the room he was in.

For hours he'd been hiding here, an abandoned building somewhere in Compton. Furious at finding the bitch-cow Adelaide gone, furious at the taint of the angel in her house, he'd sought out fresh sources of sustenance, the need to locate his Destiny beyond feverish.

But the second he'd begun to draw on the burn, invisible belts of white heat lashed at him. Crippled him.

He'd fled the whimpering man he'd chosen to feed on. Sought out a new source.

And the same thing had happened.

And again.

Weakening him every time he tried.

Something, *someone*, was stopping him.

Fury pummeled Wraif, and he'd fled until he'd found this derelict warehouse. The temptation to feast was nearly all-encompassing. The craving to locate his

206 | Lexxie Couper

Destiny too potent. Until he could figure out how to combat the unknown pissant adversary, he had to keep away from the human cattle.

He'd hid. Aching for her. Paced. Craved.

And then the soundless voice screamed in his head at the exact second he knew the fucking angel had fucked his Destiny!

Clawing at his face, he threw back his head and screamed again. "No!"

They have consummated. Their bodies have joined. They have—

"*I know!*" he roared, shutting down the soundless voice. "I know! But I don't know where she is! I don't—"

I do. I know. Now listen to me.

And he did.

Chapter Eight

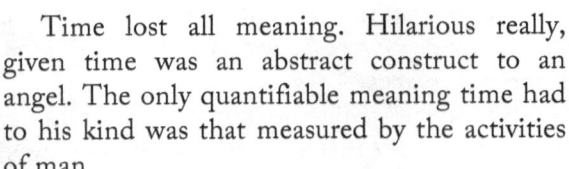

Time lost all meaning. Hilarious really, given time was an abstract construct to an angel. The only quantifiable meaning time had to his kind was that measured by the activities of man.

And in *this* activity of man, Nathanial had lost all track of time.

Being inside Billie, moving inside her, moving with her…

Time no longer existed. Only being with *her* did.

In their private world, shielded from everything else, the only thing that mattered was her pleasure, her rapture.

And in tending to that, he found his own.

For the first time in all his millennia of existence, he found *his* true pleasure.

Her eyes held his as he rolled his hips, stroking deeper into her with each thrust. She whispered his name over and over, her fingers caressing his back, the scapulars of his wings. With every touch of her fingertips on the downy axillaries, sensations unlike any he'd ever experienced shot through him, his body thrumming with an urgency both foreign and sublime.

Wing play was common among his kind during sexual interaction, and he was no untouched novice—but nothing had *ever* felt like this.

Because finally, this means something. Finally, it is not only your body, but your heart and your soul being aroused.

"Nathanial," Billie breathed again, sliding her heel up the back of his thigh, her eyes smoldering with a desire that fed his own.

The slightest of shift in position allowed him to sink deeper into her still, and molten pleasure sheared through him.

Fighting with the inevitable, knowing he was close to a release that would change everything, he cupped her face with one hand.

So close. He was so close...

He didn't want to climax before her, and with a single gossamer thread of his influence, he could make her orgasm, but he would rather burn in Satan's favorite chamber than flaw this transcendent moment by altering its truth.

Everything was the way it was meant to be, without celestial influence…and that was exactly as he wanted it.

Billie's heel dug into the base of his spine as her inner muscles squeezed him tighter. Her eyes fluttered close. Her breathing quickened, grew shallow. "I'm…I'm close…"

"I am as well," he said, the confession a tortured groan.

Her lips curled and her fingers raked over his shoulder. "G-good."

A tight tingling began in the base of his spine, intense and heady.

"Billie," he rasped, his movement growing faster, erratic. "I can't hold off any longer."

She fisted her hand in the hair at the back of his head. "Then don't."

He smiled, and then moaned as she wrapped her other leg around his hip, locked her ankles at the base of his spine and squeezed him again.

His body reacted. Took over. Control abandoned him. Or perhaps he surrendered it. Surrendered to her. To the sensations she awoke in him. Not just now, but since the first moment he'd grown aware of the light that would become her.

He surrendered to Billie. To everything she was to him, to everything she'd done to him.

In that moment, with their bodies connected in the most intimate way, holding each other's gazes, breath mingling with every panting gasp, he willingly gave himself over to her.

Just as she reached the zenith.

She cried out his name, her inner muscles contracting around him.

The world splintered. Reality shifted. He was torn apart and remade, incomprehensible pleasure rendering him his true form—a being of light—for a microsecond. Billie clawed at his back, her knuckles sliding against the root of his wings, and he was torn apart and remade yet again.

Over and over. With every constricting pulse of her inner walls around him, he was remade, his thrust wild, his breath ragged, his release a heartbeat away from eruption.

Protection.

The single word filled his head and, as he fell over the edge into a pleasure beyond him, he snatched at his last vestiges of control. Removed any chance of his release creating life.

Even as the unexpected and overwhelming longing to do so with her flooded him.

Until he, too, erupted.

And then he was little but light.

Inside her.

The light—his light—filled the room, filled

Billie. She clung to him, holding him to her, taking him deeper, even as his human form disappeared in the light. She held him and cried his name, gazed up at him, saw him— *truly* saw him.

Billie, he said, his human voice lost.

"Nathanial," she whispered, her legs still wrapped around a form no longer there, and yet there all the same. "Oh Nathanial…"

The world splintered again. Shattered. And he was human once more.

They rode out their pleasure together, until—long moments later, or even a lifetime— her legs slid from around his back and her breath left her on a wobbly laugh.

He smiled, still embedded inside her, reveling in the sated rapture in her eyes. "This is a good laugh, yes?"

Her smile stretched wider and she trailed her fingertips down his back to his butt. "This is an oh-my-God-where-have-you-been-all-my-life laugh."

He chuckled himself. "I've been with you."

"Then can we go back in time so you can be my first, please?"

His heart thumped faster in his chest.

She closed her eyes, still smiling. "Can you make it so you're my only?"

He could. With a thought, he could erase every other touch she'd ever had. But he wouldn't. Truth. He would never rob her of her truth.

"Oh God," she groaned suddenly, slapping a hand to her face. "You've been with me forever? That means you've seen every time I picked my nose?"

He arched an eyebrow.

"No!" she groaned louder.

"Kidding." He laughed. "I did look away often."

She returned her hand to his hair and gave him a stern look, even as her lips twitched. "You better have."

He chuckled again, and then sobered, brushing a knuckle along her jaw. "I did everything I could to *not* be aware of you, Billie."

She held his gaze.

He brushed her jaw again. "But you do look adorable when you pick your—"

She groaned and laughed and flipped him onto his back, and—because he was an angel— he grew hard again in a second.

And he took her to the pinnacle of sexual rapture all over again.

And again.

And again.

Until they were both spent. Drained.

A shaky laugh fell from him as he finally, reluctantly, withdrew from her body. "Now there's something I never thought could happen."

"What's that?" she asked, eyes closed, lips curled in a lazy smile, fingers trailing a slow pattern over her stomach.

"I'm actually exhausted."

"Need to up your cardio, Mr. Knight. I can't have you physically pooped every night."

Joy bloomed through him, stealing his breath. "Are you telling me you expect this every night?"

She opened one eye and looked at him. "If it's not too presumptuous."

He swallowed. "For how long?"

"How long you got?"

An eternity.

He stopped the word before it could leave his lips. Until Gilbert was caught, until the fallen responsible for the man's unnatural transformation was found and dealt with, he couldn't allow himself the luxury of dreaming. This amazing stolen moment with Billie now was all he could afford.

For an answer, he kissed her. And then kissed her collarbone, her shoulder, her breasts, her belly, and lower…

One more time of hearing her cry out his name in pleasure. One more time…

One more time turned into two more times.

The *last* time, she breathlessly laughed her

surrender, informing him she was in very real danger of dying from sexual rapture.

"I'm tapping out," she part groaned, part laughed, planting her feet on his shoulders and pushing him away. "You win."

He complied with a grin, even as his human form seemed to shake from overexertion.

He'd just inched his butt to the edge of the bed, with the intention of taking a shower, when two strong hands grabbed his shoulders and he was flattened to his back.

Billie grinned down at him, sliding her palms over his chest. "Payback."

He lost time all over again, as she did things to his body with her mouth he couldn't comprehend or resist.

Finally, after *he* cried *her* name more than once, he climbed off the bed, scooped up his discarded jeans and shoved his legs into them.

"Your wings are incredible, by the way."

His heart smashed up into his throat at her statement. Tingling, he turned and looked at her.

"I can see them." She smiled, her gaze focused on the space behind him. "They're beautiful. Majestic and amazing."

He cast a quick glance over his shoulder and flexed his wings.

"Wow," she breathed.

"I still don't understand how you can see

them," he said, frowning at her with a smile. "But I'm glad you can."

"Me too." She crossed her legs, hugged a pillow to her chest, and rested her chin on its soft edge. "They do it for me."

He flexed them again.

She grinned.

"*I* am going to make you some food," he said. If he didn't, he would climb back on the bed and make love to her again.

"And *I* will eat it." She cocked an eyebrow. "For some reason, I'm famished."

Laughing himself, he removed the barrier protecting them from the outside world.

BROTHER! I've found him! Brother!

He slammed his hands to his ears, Erah's shout smashing through his head at the very second James materialized in the room in front of him.

"It's happened again," James said, stare locked on him. "In Compton. Maybe. Somewhere near there. Nim detected a massive blast of dark— Shit, Feathers, did I interrupt a—"

Brother, I've found him!

An awareness of a location sheared through Nathanial's existence—Compton.

Get here! Get here now!

"Nathanial?" Billie's voice battled Erah's.

Worry filled James's face and he stepped

forward, reaching out for Nathanial. "What's going on, Feath—"

NOW! Erah boomed.

He swung to Billie, the location Erah kept planting in his head clouding his vision. A warehouse. Abandoned. Derelict.

"Nathanial?" She still sat on the bed, hugging the pillow tighter to her chest, worry eating up her face. "What's wrong?"

"I know where he is," he said.

She gasped.

He destroyed the distance between them in a blur, cupped her face in his hands and kissed her. "I'll be back."

"I—"

He snapped back to James. "Protect her."

"Done." James nodded. "She'll be safe. I promise."

BROTHER! Erah bellowed. *Get here NOW!*

Nathanial translocated to the warehouse.

Silence wrapped around him. Cold. Crypt-like.

He scanned the empty space, fists bunched.

Crumbling, graffiti-covered concrete pillars surrounded him. Debris covered the filthy floor. The acrid stench of human and animal defecation hung heavy in the motionless air.

Erah?

Nothing.

Erah? he called again, pivoting. This was

the location Erah had shared with him. Every molecule in his being recognized it. So where was Gilbert? Where was his brother? Why couldn't he detect a sign of either of them?

"Erah?" he called aloud.

His voice echoed around the dark warehouse, deteriorating into a wordless sound.

Nothing.

"Brother?" he called louder, turning.

Still nothing.

No, it was more than nothing. It was a void. As if he suddenly ceased to exist to anyone or anything. Even his shout no longer echoed.

Something is wrong.

The icy air pressed down on him.

Gut churning, he curled his fists tighter. It wasn't right. This wasn't right. Gilbert wasn't here, and neither was Erah.

Get back to Billie. Now.

He flexed his wings.

Ice enveloped him in a suffocating embrace.

What was going on? He strained against it. Fought to open his wings.

They couldn't move. Wouldn't move.

Erah!

His shout fell into nothingness. Into the void.

"Fuck," he murmured, a sickening realization sinking into his gut. "No. No...no."

He squinted at the floor, searching for—

"Fuck!"

The angel's snare was large, its diameter so massive it almost contained the warehouse's entire floor. So wide, he hadn't detected it until he'd tried to open his wings. Painted onto the floor with dark, thick blood, it had done exactly what it was meant to do—incarcerate an angel the precise moment he used his power.

If he hadn't tried to open his wings...

The void imprisoned him. Immobilized him. Rendered him powerless and crushed down on him.

"Fuck!"

How...*who* had done this? Gilbert? Where was Erah? Was he harmed? Had Gilbert trapped him as well? Was the unknown fallen responsible?

"Erah?" he roared, fighting against the invisible imprison.

Silence. No echo. No sound. Just the void of the angel's snare.

Until the snare was destroyed, he was trapped. And with every passing second, the snare drained him of his force. Leeched it from him, until he would be nothing but an empty shell.

A weapon against angels devised by the darkest of demons.

"Fuck," he snarled again.

He had no way of reaching Billie, or Erah,

or James. No way of reaching beyond the snare. All he could hope was for Erah to come looking for him.

If Gilbert hasn't gotten to him first.

No. It was impossible. Gilbert—or whatever Gilbert had become—was strong, but unlike Nathanial, Erah was an angel at full power. Not fallen. Not cut off from his brethren, his nourishment and sustenance.

How do you know how strong Gilbert is now? You refused to snag his threads, his wisps, for anything longer than a second. Too scared of what his lust for Billie would do to you. Too scared to do your job properly.

Scrunching up his face, he tried to move.

Ice crushed him. Crippled him.

He grew still, calm. Drew a slow breath.

I know You have cast me out. I know I have defied You. He sent the prayer out into the void, an exercise in desperate futility. His Creator no longer acknowledged his existence, after all. *But please, my Lord, I need—*

"Knight?"

He snapped his eyes open at the faint shout.

"Knight, are you here?"

His heart slammed against his breastbone.

"Kade?" The vampire's name left him on a cracked whisper. Ice poured into his open mouth, down his throat.

Fight it. Fight. It.

"Kade."

The void roped around him. Fed the ice. Ground down on him.

Fight.

IT.

"Kade!"

His shout bounced around the empty warehouse. Fell into silence.

Kade! he bellowed in his mind.

"Knight?" A dark blur cut the space, and suddenly Kade stood before him. "What's—"

"Angel's...sn-snare," Nathanial ground out, the words barely a strangled rasp. "Need...break...barrier..."

Piercing green eyes drilled into him. Confusion flittered over the man's seamless face.

Fighting the icy void, Nathanial forced his stare to the warehouse's floor. "Des...troy...the...sn..."

Kade moved, a dark blur streaking toward the far wall of the warehouse.

The ice sank into Nathanial's bones. Agony screamed through him, his wings, his soul.

And then—his body moved. Crumpling to the floor, gasping.

A strong, cold hand gripped his upper arm, catching his fall. Halting it. "In here, Nim!" Kade's deep shout reverberated around the warehouse. "I've found him."

Nathanial struggled to lift his head. It was as if someone had dropped a planet on the back of his neck.

"Who did this to you, Knight?" Kade asked, his grip on Nathanial's arm tightening. "Are you okay?"

Weak. So weak. He could hardly stand, let alone return to Billie. How was he to get back to her, find out what was going on, where Erah was, where Gilbert was, if he could hardly—

"Crap, Knight." A petite woman with a bright purple buzz cut stumbled to a halt directly in front of him. "What happened?" Eyes wide, she touched his chest—and jerked it away with a sharp hiss. "Angel's snare," she said, flicking an angry glare at Kade.

Kade frowned. "I don't know what that is."

Nim looked back at Nathanial. "It traps angels. Imprisons them. Drains them of their force until they're empty husks. Dark, parasitic magic. The darkest. Requires not only blood sacrifice, but souls. Innocents suffer to execute it. Nasty stuff. Only a powerful force can wield it, and even then the personal toll is dreadful."

"Who did this to him?"

Nim shook her head. "I don't know. I haven't seen anything like this." She frowned up at Kade. "You broke the circle?"

"The blood ring? Yes." Kade dipped his head, his green eyes fixed on Nathanial. Worry shone in them, an unusual emotion for the owner of the agency. The ancient vampire rarely showed any emotion considered favorable or compassionate. "Now I want to know who did this to Knight so I can rip out their throat and watch their own life drain from them."

"I don't..." Nathanial shook his head. "I need to..." Fuck, he felt as feeble as a newborn human babe. A cold shudder rocked through him. Pain lanced up his wings. He groaned, his knees giving out.

"Whoa there, big guy." Kade hoisted him upward again, steadying him on his feet. "What do you need us to do?"

Nathanial shook his head again. He had to get back to Billie.

Erah? He reached out for the other angel.

Silence.

Was his brother okay?

"I'm alright." He tapped Kade's hand, all too aware his own shook.

The vampire slowly let him go. And caught him the second he crumpled again.

"Yeah. I can see that." Kade flicked Nim another look. "I want the being responsible for this. *Now.*"

"Sure, boss. I hear you." Nim frowned at Nathanial. "But first..." She stepped forward and, eyes closing, touched Nathanial's chest again.

A warm ribbon unfurled through his body from the contact, melting a path through the ice trying to devour him, filling the hungry void with heat.

Nim's heat. The heat of a white wiccan.

"What are you doing?" Kade asked, his hand still around Nathanial's arm.

"Giving him a top-up. Kinda." She smiled at Nathanial. "That'll help. A little. Until you can—"

"Billie," Nathanial mumbled. The heat spread through him faster. Through the void. "I need to get to Billie."

"The human James told us about?" Kade's eyes narrowed. "Is she in trouble?"

Nathanial flexed his wings.

"This is the second time you've…" Heat filled Billie's cheeks, and she hugged the pillow closer to her chest, arching an eyebrow at James. "Y'know."

Her brain, still struggling to process the fact Nathanial had vanished a few minutes ago, was furiously reminding her the only thing covering her birthday suit was said pillow.

James, now at the large window, one hand pressed to the glass, the other rubbing at the back of his neck, tossed her a look over his shoulder. "Shite. Sorry."

The softest of touch caressed her skin as a

pair of jeans and a loose white linen shirt materialized on her body.

"Whoa." She scrambled off the bed and looked down at herself.

"Do they fit?" He frowned. "Women's sizes have always tripped me up. Every bloody country is different. A six here is completely different to a six in, say, New Zealand."

"They fit." And they did. Perfectly. The faded jeans were the most comfortable she'd ever worn, and the shirt, while loose and baggy, hung from her shoulders with stylish perfection. Throw on a killer pair of heels and some flashy jewelry and she'd have no problem attending a fan convention or industry event.

He nodded and turned back to the window. Outside, the day was summer perfection. Not a cloud marred the blue sky and towering trees reached for the Heavens. Just where was Nathanial's home located if she could see city lights from one side and what looked like a forest from the other?

Another one of those questions she really needed answers to.

"Thank you," she said to James's back. "For the clothes. And for helping Nathanial." She pinched her thumbnail. "I wish I could. I feel powerless."

The confession left her on a wobbly sigh. Getting magically dressed by a genie should be cause for excitement. Of course, when it happened because the angel she loved had—

Loved?

"Oh God," she muttered. "That's inconvenient."

"You're not powerless," James said, turning from the vista beyond the window. "Just…a little out of your league at the moment. It's all good though. I suspect after this, Feathers will give you a crash course in all sorts of defense techniques suitable for combatting…nonhumans." He frowned. "And what's inconvenient? Do you need something? Remember, I'm a pro at getting whatever you want."

Could he get her a new heart? One to replace the stupid one she had now? Falling in love with an angel…how was this ever going to end well?

"Bill?"

She blinked.

James stood beside her, worry knitting his eyebrows. "You okay? Feathers will erase me from existence—well, try to—if you're anything less than the way he left you, and I'd hate to disappoint him." A small smile danced on his lips for a second. "You're not allowed to tell him that, right?"

"I'm okay." Just stupid. And in love. Maybe. Oh God, what the hell was wrong with her?

"Concerned, is all."

He narrowed his eyes. "For an actress, you're a woeful liar."

She snorted, even as her heart thumped harder in her throat. "You'd be surprised how dissimilar the two actually are."

More worry crossed his face.

"Question?" She dropped back down onto the bed.

He joined her, sitting beside her. "Sure. Hit me. Figuratively, not literally."

She rolled her eyes.

He grinned, and then nudged her shoulder with his. "Go on. I'm all ears."

"Do many... Is it possible..." God, how did she ask this? *Why* was she asking this? "Can..." Damn it.

"Can humans and nonhumans be in a relationship?" he said.

"How did you know that's what I wanted to ask?"

He smiled. "As I said earlier, I'm brilliant at reading people."

She cocked another eyebrow at him. "Is there *anything* you're not awesome or brilliant or amazing at?"

"Hmmm, let me think..." He grinned again. "Now, as for your unspoken question—"

Something unseen slammed into him, flinging him backward across the bed.

"My Destiny," a guttural voice rasped. "I finally found you!"

Billie scrambled back on the bed, stare locked on the short man standing in the bedroom doorway, his light brown hair matted—oh God, was that blood?—his pudgy face filthy with dirt, his feverish brown eyes fixed on her.

Oh no. Oh God, no!

"My Destiny." He smiled, or maybe he bared his teeth, and began walking toward her. "I'm here for you."

She scrambled back farther, flailing behind her. "J-James? James?"

What had happened to the djinn? What—

The man quickened his pace.

Heart thrashing in her ears, she reeled backwards again. Shit, was he drooling?

"Gilbert?" she burst out, searching for James with a swinging hand. "Are you Gilbert?"

"*I am Wraif!*" he screeched, face red. Baleful yellow light flared in his eyes. "*Your Wraif!*"

Heat rushed at her, like a blast from an open oven. She gasped, flinching at the gust. And then screamed when the heat turned into excruciating hot bands circling her wrists.

Gilbert's eyes blazed brighter yellow. "Come here."

The invisible bands on her wrist yanked her forward.

"No!" She thrashed against the violent pull, heels sliding on the duvet. "*No!*"

Face burning redder, he bared his teeth. "You're *mine*." Hot bands snaked around her arms, her calves.

"Fuck you!" She clawed at the duvet. Her heels slid on the bed again. "*Fuck you.*"

Gilbert shook his head, so close to the bed his stench filled her nose; stale sweat and charred meat and something else. Something older. Darker. "No, my Destiny. This is not you. This is the angel speaking. He's corrupted you. But I can cleanse you. I can—"

A thick arm of bruised-purple smoke—roiling and billowing over and over itself—smashed into his chest, flinging him backward into the wall.

"Hit a djinn when he's not looking, will you?" James materialized at the end of the attacking pillar of smoke, hair whipping back from his face, fists bunched at his side.

The angry smoke reared back and, swelling thicker and darker, punched into Gilbert's chest again.

"*No!*" the man squealed, although he didn't look like a man anymore. His face leaked blood, his teeth gnashed against his lacerated lips. Pummeled against the wall by the pole of smoke, his body flapped and convulsed, his limbs—somehow elongated and uneven—

flailing about. "Mine!"

"Run, Bill," James barked over his shoulder, eyes wide, sweat pouring down his face. "Get out of—"

A wall of red haze engulfed James, and he screamed, head back, spine bowed.

"*Mine.*" The thing once Gilbert shoved away from the wall, yellow eyes fixed on him.

Red haze rushed at James again. His body shook, twisted. His mouth moved in a silent cry.

Get

away

Bill

Billie flung herself from the bed. What did she do? She grabbed at the lamp on the side table, tearing its cord from the wall. She had to stop Gilbert. She had to—

Get

away

B—

James dropped to the floor, motionless.

"My Destiny." Gilbert smiled at her, stepping over his body.

"I'm not fucking yours!" She hoisted the lamp above her head. *Oh Nathanial, I need you. I need help.* "Get away from me."

He shook his head, eyes flickering back to brown. Confusion etched his face. "I sold my *soul* for you." He took another step toward her, holding out his hands. "I gave everything for you. Because I love you. And you love me. You have to! That's the way it's meant to be. That's what I was promised."

"I don't." Clammy ice crawled over her flesh. She inched backward, a choked whimper falling from her when her butt hit the bedside table. "I don't—"

"*That's what I was promised!*" he screamed, eyes yellow again.

"*I don't care!*" she screamed back.

Heat crashed into her, shoving her into the table. She dropped the lamp.

Oh God, it hurt. It hurt so much!

Nathanial. Nathanial, h—

The air splintered, flared into a million pinpoints of frenzied lights, and Nathanial burst into the room and charged at Gilbert.

Rammed him backward. Smashed him into the wall.

"*No!*" Rage contorted Gilbert's face. He writhed, lashing out.

And then a deafening roar filled the room and Nathanial arced backward, as if hit by an invisible blow.

Billie ran to him, wrapping her arms around his torso. "I got you. I got you."

She staggered under his weight, flinching as a blast of furnace-hot air struck her.

Nathanial groaned and righted himself. The

air shimmered, and Billie felt his wings snap open *through* her. A rush of giddy power stole her breath. Her heart slammed into her throat—and then she cried out as Nathanial slumped again.

She grabbed him. God, why was he shaking so much? It was as if he had no energy.

"Drained..." he slurred, pushing himself upright, just as Gilbert charged at them.

Nathanial spun to face Billie, hauling her to his body. She sensed his wings flex wide, and then he arched, a roar of pain tearing from him. The stench of burning feathers flooded her breath.

And still Nathanial held her, protected her.

I will never let him hurt you, his voice whispered in her head, as his stare found hers. *Never*.

He turned.

Whatever he did, Gilbert screamed in agony.

And then another wall of invisible fire hit them. Nathanial staggered back a step. Billie grabbed him.

"Stop," she screamed at Gilbert. "Stop it. St—"

"*ENOUGH!*"

A male voice boomed, deep and powerful. The heat evaporated. Sound vanished. A blinding white flooded the room, flooded everything.

"Enough," the voice said again. And suddenly a man appeared, stepping out of the light. Born from it.

Pristine white wings flexed behind him, the feathers full and flawless, the span wide and majestic. His eyes shone with an iridescent white glow, and his white shirt and pants seemed to radiate with the same light.

"Erah," Nathanial groaned. And yet, as Billie held him, his entire body began to thrum, to heat. His muscles tensed, grew harder. The smell of burning feathers vanished. "Brother."

"She's *mine!*" Gilbert screeched, staring at Erah. "You can't take her from me! I found her. I came here. I *fought* the angel! And now she's mine. Mine! You promised she'd be mine! You said—"

He disintegrated.

"Ah, fuck," Erah muttered in the silence, dropping his head to gaze at the floor.

"Wh-what?" Billie blinked. She held on to Nathanial's arm, his side. Beneath her palms, his body continued to thrum, even as he grew still. Motionless.

"Fuck," Erah muttered again.

Flicking a glance at the spot Gilbert had been standing, bile rose up in her throat. All that was left of the geography teacher stalking her was a messy scattering of dark dust on the carpet.

A life, a human, gone. Just like that.

Near the smudge, James remained motionless. Was he breathing? Did djinn breathe? Was he dead? Would Nathanial be able to resurrect him?

"Erah?"

She gripped Nathanial's arm tighter, the low rumble of his voice catching her breath. The air around him—around them both—seemed to crackle and arc.

The other angel lifted his head, his smile brilliant. Beatific. "Brother." He slid his gaze to her, and her skin crawled. "We saved the human. Together."

Nathanial's muscles coiled under her hands. "What did he mean, *you promised*?"

Erah's smile stretched wider. "The human was just gibbering. Scared. Insane. Whoever orchestrated his metamorphosis into the demon he'd become must be hunted down. Punished. We will do it together, Nathanial. Like old times. Whoever it is must be found, no matter how long it takes us. Together, *we* will find—"

"What did he mean," Nathanial repeated. "*You promised*?"

The air crackled again. Every hair on Billie's body stood at attention. Her teeth began to ache. Her pulse turned into a cannon, pounding in her ears.

Erah smiled again.

Billie bit down on the inside of her mouth. Every time he smiled, she wanted to throw up.

The subtle smell of ozone threaded into her breath, as if a fierce, unseen electrical storm raged around them. And yet the only things moving were Nathanial's muscles—coiling, stiffening—and Erah.

Ice-blue stare locked on Nathanial, he tossed his head toward the dust particles that once were Gilbert. "Humans are so stupid. I've never understood why they are His favored ones."

"What. Did. He. Mean?" The words left Nathanial on a low growl. The windows rattled with each one.

Billie swallowed, scanning the room. What would hurt an angel? What could she hit Erah with?

Hit? Why…what are you thinking?

She didn't know. But something wasn't right. This angel was almost too gorgeous to look at, her brain couldn't process it, and yet…

He was the angel she'd seen Nathanial talking to before, the one helping him find Gilbert. So why did it sound like Nathanial was about to rip him apart?

And why did she feel ill every time he looked at her?

Closing his eyes, Erah rubbed at the back of

his neck and let out a slow breath. "You weren't meant to come back here, brother."

Nathanial stiffened. "What?"

Erah shook his head and smiled at Nathanial. "So unlike you to accept help. I wasn't prepared for it."

"What did you do?" Nathanial took a step toward him, even as he held his arms out and back toward Billie. The windows rattled again. Ozone tainted the air, thick and ripe and charged.

"The snare was meant to keep you there, in that piss-drenched building." A disgusted expression twisted Erah's beautiful face. "Until I came to save you."

"Erah…" Nathanial stepped forward. The walls creaked. Every object in the room vibrated, as if agitated. Or frenzied. "Please tell me you're not—"

"Of course I'm the one who fucking did it!"

Billie pressed her palm to her mouth. Her eyes burned. She stared at the other angel, bile rising in her throat.

"Why?" Shock filled Nathanial's voice.

"*Why?*" Erah threw up his hands. "You chose a pathetic human over *me*. You threw away everything, you threw away *us*. For her." Ice-blue eyes snapped to Billie and she shrank away from the hate burning in their depths. "You weren't supposed to do that."

A low growl tore from Nathanial's chest. His shoulders hunched, fists balling. "You *wanted* Gilbert to find Billie?"

"Of course I did. I've been patient, brother. I allowed you time down here, wallowing. But when I finally realized you weren't going to see the error of your ways and beg His forgiveness to return to where you belong, I had to influence things a little. When I discovered a man willing to do *anything* to be with this quim, I set the ball rolling. "

A cold fist twisted in Billie's chest.

Erah flicked her another look. His top lip curled. "He was supposed to get to her before you intervened. But I was caught up in some insignificant shit *He* ordered me to do, and I couldn't get to you in time. Gilbert was meant to take her, fuck her until her brain was nothing but mush and she no longer existed— mentally or physically—in this realm. But you got to her first, brought her here, and I had to figure out how to sep—"

An unseen explosion destroyed every object in the room. The bedside tables shattered, sending splinters flying. The windows broke. The TV screen erupted in a violent shower of glass shards.

Billie screamed, ducking.

Nathanial's wings snapped wide.

Erah staggered backward, eyes bulging.

"Wait wait *wait*, brother!" He gaped at the debris showering down on them, hands out. "Think about this. Really think about it! She's *human*. Nothing but a meat popsicle with a tiny brain and a set of tits! She will *never* make you whole or complete the way I—"

Erah flew backward into the wall.

Red. Everything—red.

Through the red haze, Nathanial watched Erah slam into the wall. Watched him fall to his knees, stumble back onto his feet, raise a hand toward him. "Brother."

The red haze grew darker at Erah's groaned plea.

End him.

"Jealousy," Nathanial whispered. "You did all this because of *jealousy*?"

He'd used the little energy Nim had given him at the warehouse to translocate back home. Drained of almost all his force, he'd been on the cusp of collapse during his battle with Gilbert. Had been ready to die to stop the geography teacher from getting to Billie. Would have, he suspected.

He'd been prepared for that.

But not this.

My brother, my fellow angel...

He stared at Erah, now standing upright again, wings alert. Charged power radiated from Erah, and Nathanial fed from it. Drank it in. He may not have been prepared for Erah's betrayal, but he doubted Erah had been prepared for *this*. Two angels, facing off.

No, Erah would not have anticipated this. And there was nothing he could do to stop Nathanial from drawing on his power.

Except kill him.

Will he go that far?

Frowning at Erah, he shook his head. "You put the woman I love in danger because you...what? Wanted your brother back?" He began walking forward, bunching his fists. "Innocent people died because you missed our conversations?"

"You were *mine!*" Erah shouted. "Not *hers*. You were meant to only ever want *me*."

Icy disbelief sheared through Nathanial. "*Want* you? Erah, you are my—"

Erah's sword materialized in his hand.

"Nathanial!" Billie screamed, as the blade erupted in blue flame.

"Erah, stop." This could not be happening.

Erah shook his head. The sword's flame flickered in his eyes, blue rage burning in blue insanity. "You just need the problem removed, my brother. Let me do it for you. She won't suffer for long, and then you can return to me."

Rage seared through Nathanial's disbelief. The world turned red again. Incapable of drawing his own sword—denied it by God for falling for Billie—he held his arms wide. The only weapon he had against Erah was his physical body and the force pulled from the other angel. If he disarmed him, he might stand a chance, but only until Erah held his sword again.

The power—and weakness—of the angel sword: only the angel it was created for could wield it. It meant an enemy could never use the weapon to kill, but it also meant another angel could not use it in battle.

Damn it, if only he'd shared his location with Kade and Nim.

He reached out in his mind for James...and ground his teeth.

Heavy darkness roped through the Order of Actuality where James's existence should be.

Waves of cold fear and anger rolled over him from behind.

Billie. Still behind him. He had to get her out of here. Away from Erah. But how?

Erah smiled over Nathanial's shoulder. "I feel your fear, little human. It'll be okay. It's better you no longer—"

Nathanial threw himself at Erah. Drove his shoulder into his chest and rammed him backward into the wall again.

The solid plane of Erah's chest vanished and Nathanial smashed into the wall for a split second before chasing Erah's unseen existence.

There.

He spun, kicking the re-emerging angel to his knees just as Erah swung his sword at Billie.

Billie squealed, ducked, and drove her heel into Erah's face.

Erah jerked backward, his sword flinging from grip and disappearing.

Nathanial snagged his arm and hauled him around, crunching his fist into Erah's jaw.

"Fuck!" Erah roared, and blasted a wave of energy at Nathanial.

No.

Planting his feet, Nathanial leaned into the force, feeding on it. His blood roared in his ears. His body thrummed.

Did Erah not realize what he was doing? Did he care?

...endherkillher...

Erah's feverish thought pummeled him, as did image after vivid image of Billie screaming in agony, impaled by Erah's flaming sword.

"No!" he screamed, hurling a wall of force at Erah. And another. Another.

With a shriek, Erah blurred through the air with preternatural speed and slammed Nathanial to the floor.

Something splintered inside Nathanial's torso. Pain ripped through him. He struck out, smashing his fist into Erah's jaw again, following the physical blow with an invisible strike of raw force.

Erah flew backward, wings flailing, arms and legs doing the same, before he hit the floor near the bed with a thud.

"You need to stop this, Erah!" Nathanial growl, climbing to his feet.

Fresh pain lanced down his side. Up into his neck. He pressed his palm to his ribs. Broken rib. No, two.

Great. He needed to finish this. Now.

"I've never been—"

Erah threw both hands up into the air and down, and Nathanial's knees buckled beneath him.

"*Yes,*" Erah shouted. "You have. From the beginning!"

Willing his body, his wings, to work, Nathanial launched himself upright. "I will die trying to stop you. You must know that."

"This isn't how it was meant to be, my brother." The air cracked, and once again, Erah's sword appeared in his hand. Ignited. "You'll realize that when I remove the human stain from your mind and heart. I know you will!"

Behind him, Billie scrambled over to James. Shook him.

The djinn didn't move.

Erah started to turn, and Nathanial sent a

jolt of force into his side. "If you even look at Billie again, Erah, I will rip out your eyes!"

"You see what she has done to you?" Erah shook his head, turning back to him. Grief and disgust etched his face. "The Nathanial I have loved since the beginning of creation would never say something like that to me."

Nathanial bunched his shoulder. "This isn't love, Erah. You're wrong. This? What you're feeling? It's obsession."

The sword's flames burned brighter, eating the air with blue hunger. "No, Gilbert Sanders was obsessed. I am *nothing* like him. His obsession allowed him to become a monster. My love will save you from a worthless existence. Return you to the exalted status you deserve."

"Do you hear yourself, Erah?"

Erah smiled. "I do. And you do, as well. I know you do. What we had? Together? It's there, waiting for you again. All you need to do is let me remove the stain from existence." His eyes flared white light. "Or do it yourself."

Nathanial flicked a look around the room. Billie couldn't get away, no matter how much he wanted her gone. Erah stood between her and the door, and he wouldn't let her leave. Wouldn't stop until he'd killed her. Nathanial had to get Erah away from *her*. There was no other option. Erah would continue until she was dead.

He needed to…to…

What?

A dismayed chill twisted in his gut. Drawing a deep breath, he focused on Erah. "If I promise to give myself to you, you'll leave Billie alone?"

"Nathanial!" Horror filled Billie's moan. "Don't. You can't! I'm not worth it."

Ignoring her, Nathanial stepped closer to Erah. "I'll give myself to you, Erah. Willingly. Be everything you want me to be. I swear. But you must let Billie go. I will forget her. I will be yours. But only if you let her go. *Now.*"

Erah's nostrils flared. He ran his gaze over Nathanial, eyes white, sword burning brighter.

Nathanial moved closer still. "I *will* be yours, brother," he repeated. "But please…let her go."

"No!" Billie cried, gripping James's inert shoulder. "No, please don't—"

"Shhh," Erah hushed her, without breaking eye contact with Nathanial.

Inches away, Nathanial stopped. "I promise."

And he did. With every fiber of his existence, he did. For Billie's safety, for her life, he would give his freedom and *his* life.

Whatever I need to do. For her…

"I swear," he said, holding Erah's gaze.

Erah frowned. Searching his eyes, he reached up and cupped Nathanial's face in one hand. "Forever?"

Nathanial dipped his head.

Erah smiled, snaring a fistful of Nathanial's hair in a vise grip. "Say it. Say 'I'm yours and only yours, my brother.'"

"I'm yours," the words scratched at Nathanial's soul. "And only yours, my brother."

"As it should be." Erah smiled wider, his grip on Nathanial's hair slackening. "As it will always be." He paused, gaze tracing Nathanial's lips. "But you've been inside her, my love." His eyes turned inky black as the sword in his hand erupted in roaring black flames. "So I have no choice but to kill her."

He yanked Nathanial forward, crushed his lips in a savage kiss, filling Nathanial's mind with an image of Erah sinking his flaming sword between Billie's breasts, and then spun to face her.

"Die, cunt," Erah snarled.

At the very second Nathanial's own sword materialized in his hand.

It's Yours, a Voice declared in his head. *The* Voice.

The sword's devastating, cataclysmic power radiated up Nathanial's arm, into his body. His soul.

His sword.

Yours, the Voice said. *Again.* "Brother," he said, grabbing Erah's shoulder and swinging him back around to face him.

Their eyes met, locked—as Nathanial buried his sword to the hilt in Erah's chest.

It wouldn't kill him, but it would render him—

Brilliant white flame erupted around the blade, licked up Erah's chest, burst from his back, and engulfed his wings. His eyes blazed back to white, his stare on Nathanial, his mouth agape.

Nathanial's heart smashed up into his throat. How was this... It wasn't possible. It wasn't—

"B-but, I love you," Erah rasped, grabbing at Nathanial's wrist. "I...love..."

His hand slipped off. His wings burned. The deafening boom of his sword falling to his feet filled the room.

Nathanial held his shoulder, and tightened his grip on his own sword, his heart tearing apart as Erah's eyes flickered back to normal light blue again.

"I love you," Erah repeated on a whisper, fingertips brushing at Nathanial's jaw, his mouth. "You're m...mine..."

The flame of Nathanial's sword flared brighter. Whiter.

Erah's eyes widened. His fingers clawed at

Nathanial's shoulder, his chest. *I'm sorry*, he mouthed, as the flame consumed him. *I'm—*

He vanished.

As did Nathanial's sword and its white fire.

"I'm sorry," Nathanial echoed on a whisper, dropping to his knees.

He landed on a pillow. A pillow that hadn't been there a second before.

"It's the best," a croaky voice rasped from across the room, "I could do."

"James?" Billie gasped, shaking the djinn again.

"I'm…alive…" James waved a shaky hand in the air before letting it thud back to the floor. "I think."

Nathanial slumped, stared at Billie and the moaning djinn for a heartbeat, and closed his eyes.

Erah? he called, reaching out.

Silence.

Beyond silence. Nothing.

Where once the vivacious thread of Erah's existence colored the Order of Actuality, now…emptiness.

Raw pain sliced through Nathanial, and he scrunched up his face. An angel's sword could only injure another angel, unless it burned fire. Then…it killed.

God? Have You done this? Is this Your will?

Silence.

"Nathanial?"

He lifted his head at Billie's whisper.

She lowered herself to the floor in front of him. Worry ate up her face. She reached out a hand, her fingertips brushing his jaw, and pulled away. Her gaze moved to his wings, and she frowned.

"Can you still see them?"

"Yes."

Relief rushed through him at her answer. For some reason, he didn't like the idea of her no longer being able to see that which she was never meant to see in the first place. "How do they look?"

A soft chuckle fell from her. "Ruffled."

He snorted, the sound weak and wobbly. "I suspect that's an understatement."

"You still look handsome, you winged bastard," James called from the floor, flopping his hand above his head, eyes closed.

Billie smiled and touched Nathanial's jaw again. "Are you okay?"

Was he? Could he be?

Sucking in a breath, he nodded. "Are you?"

"Well, I just witnessed a genie and a...whatever Gilbert had become fight, a man disintegrate in front of me, and two angels..." She stopped, shaking her head. "Nope. Can't joke my way out of this one. I think I might be a little screwed up."

"I'm sorry, Billie."

She frowned at him. "Is this your fault?"

"Erah—"

She shook her head, and fixed a level look on him. "Did you control what Erah did? Did you make him seek out Gilbert, change him? Did you ever say to him, 'Hey Erah, how 'bout you and I spend forever together and to hell with anyone else'?"

"This lecture sounds a little familiar." It did. He'd given her a similar one about Gilbert only…what? The day before? How much of her life had changed now? And his?

She shrugged, her smile wry. "Well, it was a good lecture. Worthy of being heeded."

"Was it now?"

"Yes."

He swallowed. He wanted to take her in his arms. Hold her. Kiss her. Tell her everything was going to be okay.

But he couldn't.

He'd ended the existence of an angel in front of a human. His sword had been returned to him and he'd used it to end his brother.

He had no idea how *everything* was going to be now. Not at all.

Then make use of the moments you have. Make the best of—

He threaded his fingers into her hair and kissed her.

Gave everything he was to her. His heart, his soul, his love.

Everything.

She wrapped her arms around his neck and kissed him back, caressing the edges of his wings.

Pleasure and joy rolled through Nathanial, mingling with the despair gnawing at him. A life without Billie stretched before him. Empty and soulless and without purpose. He would remember every second he'd spent with her. Every laugh and frown and sarcastic quip.

He kissed her and, as her lips moved over his, he slipped into her mind and healed the trauma of it all.

She wouldn't forget, but it would never give her nightmares. Nothing mattered right at that moment, not the inexplicable return of his sword, not the fact he'd killed Erah, nothing except knowing Billie would never be traumatized by what she'd just experienced.

Perhaps you need to make her forget you as well? It would be for the best if you never existed to her.

She pulled away and scowled fiercely. "Don't even *think* about it, Knight."

He blinked. "What?"

"Don't even think about making me forget you. And I don't know where you think you're going, but I'm going with you."

"Billie." He closed his eyes. "You can't. I'm not human. And you're—"

"In love with you." She tilted her chin and glared up at the ceiling. "And if whoever's in charge up there doesn't like it, well…He, She, It…can bite me!"

"Bite…" He buried his hand in her hair again and kissed her harder. Lost himself to her.

Maybe for the last time. Any second now, he would be removed from this plane of existence. God had returned his sword to him, but the fallout from Erah's actions would rock Heaven for an eternity. The repercussions would be far-reaching.

The fact that Erah had hidden his state of mind, his actions from Nathanial for so long was unsettling, but then, Nathanial *was* a fallen. So much of his old existence was now denied him.

That Erah had kept it from those higher on the hierarchy, however, was astounding.

Would God allow Billie to keep her memories? Could Nathanial convince Him to leave her alone?

She Will Only Be Alone If You Deem Her To Be So.

The deep, calm voice filled Nathanial's head.

The One voice. *His* voice.

Pulled away from Billie, he stared at her.

"What?" she said.

You Have A Choice To Make, Nathanial.

Nathanial drew a deep breath. *A choice? What kind of choice?*

The particles in the room swirled and shifted, and Nathanial's sword appeared once more, hanging blade down in the air beside him.

Heart pounding, he studied it.

It Is My Will For You To Have It Again. Take Your Sword, And Resume Your Place In Heaven.

Heaven. His home. His old life.

He swallowed.

"Nathanial?" Billie whispered. "Are you okay?"

He looked at her. At his sword. At her.

Her. His reason for drawing breath. His purpose now.

Take The Sword, Nathanial. There was a pause. A silent offering. *Or Don't.*

"I choose don't," he whispered. cupping Billie's face. "I choose life with her."

Good Choice, the deep, calm voice said. *I Approve.*

Nathanial smiled, gazing into Billie's eyes. *Why am I not surprised?*

There was a cavernous laugh. *I'm Omnipotent, Remember? Most Of The Time.*

Why can Billie can see my wings? Why can she

hear me speak Enochian? Did you do that?

Sometimes, I Feel Like Bestowing Something Special Upon Those I Love.

Nathanial's throat thickened. Such a simple explanation, but it said so much.

And yet... Swallowing, he frowned. *Did you know? What Erah was doing?*

I Was Aware Of The Intensity Of Your Brother's Emotions For You, But I Hoped He Would Not Succumb To Them.

Is he—

Be Well, Nathanial. I Will Be Watching.

A rush of golden rapture flooded through Nathanial. His wings flexed. Fluffed. And tucked back into their restful position. Not gone. But restored to their full strength and splendor.

He laughed, enough for Billie to frown. "Want to tell me what's going on? Anything to do with the sword floating in the air a moment ago? And the fact your wings seemed to get a some kind of upgrade before shimmering out of sight?"

His sword, his wings... So many things Billie should never have been aware of, and yet she was. Clearly *God* had known so much more than what was going on all along. His sword never would have been returned to him if it hadn't been God's will. Of course, Nathanial would get no answers if he asked. Things didn't work that way up there. And really, the only answer he needed was currently kneeling in front of him, eyebrows dipped in a slight frown.

"I just found out I'm welcome back into Heaven," he said.

She grew still. "Oh. So you're not…a *fallen* angel anymore?"

He smiled. "I'm not."

"Oh." She pulled away a little. "So you're a full angel again?"

"I am." The potency of his life force surged through him. A rush rivaled only by his feelings for her.

"So that means you're—"

"Staying right here." He laced his fingers through hers. "With you. If you're okay with—"

She launched herself at him. Flattened him to the floor. Kissed him.

Until he groaned with a desire so deep and absolute, the endless entirety of his soul shook.

"Hello," James called. "I'm still here."

With another groan, Nathanial rolled Billie onto her back and tore his lips from hers. "Are you dying, Jimmy?"

"Let me check." A pause. "No."

"Do you need an angel to help you?" Nathanial raked his gaze over Billie's face. She grinned. God, he loved how her eyes twinkled with mischief. How her whole face lit up with playful delight.

"Let me check again," James called back. Another pause. "No. Again."

Nathanial smiled at Billie. "Then sod off, djinn."

"Okay." Laughter threaded through James's answer.

Nathanial grinned. "Oh, and Jimmy?"

"Yeah, Feathers?"

"Thank you." He brushed his thumb over Billie's bottom lip. "Seriously, thank you. For keeping the woman I love safe."

A low chuckle wafted over from the floor. "Remember that when I tell you it's your turn to clean out the office fridge."

"I like him," Billie murmured, lips curling. "Can we keep him?"

Nathanial laughed and kissed her again.

"Ummmm," James said, voice sheepish. "Maybe I *do* need an angel's help, after all."

Nathanial looked up at James, now standing beside them. "You look battered and weary, my friend."

"I took on a demonic stalker psychopath powered by jealousy. Of course I'm weary." He scrubbed at his chin. "And apparently I can't currently, y'know, *poof* away." He made an exploding gesture with his hands and ducked his head with a contrite grin. "Sorry."

Nathanial rolled his eyes and, with a smile

and a wave of his hand, returned James to the Guarded Souls office.

Billie narrowed her eyes. "Can you do that kind of thing with anyone, or just nonhumans?"

"Why?"

"There's a TV critic who really ticks me—"

He silenced her with a kiss.

"Okay, maybe just with the trash then," she murmured when he moved his lips to her throat. "If that's allowed."

"We'll talk about it after," he said, sliding his hand down her side and back up to her breast.

She lifted an eyebrow, legs wrapping around his hips. "After what?"

He grinned.

"Ever considered the joys of sharing a shower with an angel?"

Epilogue

Deanna Rhames rolled onto her side and looked at the place where her husband had slept for the last twenty-five years.

He wasn't there. He never would be again.

"I miss you, bear," she whispered, brushing her fingertips over his pillow.

Her soul ached. Her heart did as well. Would it ever stop? The pain? Would it ever go away?

A tear slipped from her eye, as it had every morning, every night since Roanon had been killed.

"I miss you so much. I can't do it. I can't go on like this. I can't...not without you. There's no... I just can't."

She couldn't. It hurt too much.

Today. Today she would take the pain away.

From her soul, and from their little girls' souls.

Take the pain and the hurt away, end it forever.

She brushed her fingers over Roanon's pillow again. "Today, bear. I'll see you later to…"

The softest sound of feathered wings kissed the air—and with it, something warm flowed through her.

Hope. Strength.

And a certainty it was going to be okay. It was all going to be okay.

Pulling a deep breath, Deanna gazed at Roanon's pillow, pictured him lying on it, smiling at her.

"I'll see you soon, bear." Her own smile stretched her lips, as warm as the new hope in her soul. "I will. But not today."

She climbed from her bed and went to wake her girls. Today was the most perfect day to go to the park.

Epilogue 2

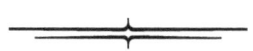

James materialized in the Guarded Souls kitchen, perfectly seated on one of the chairs at the table in the center of the room. Stark naked.

"Funny bastard, Feathers," he muttered, shaking his head.

Nim blinked at him—a fork twirled with noodles halfway to her mouth. "Does this mean Nath is okay? I've been stress eating ever since he translocated out of the warehouse in Compton."

James dressed with a click of his fingers—jeans, a white shirt, and bright red Chucks—and made a bowl of spicy Singapore noodles appear in his hand. "Feathers is fine. I left him snogging on the floor with the love of his life."

Nim grunted. "Ah, to be so lucky to have

found love, 'eh?"

James let out a wry laugh, even as his heart began to thump faster. "Yeah, if only."

He looked at the noodles in his hand, and replaced them with a Scotch egg. A favorite treat from a life he'd once had, shared with a woman forever denied him.

Shite, why did he have to go and think about *her*?

"If only," he repeated, before making the Scotch egg disappear.

Pushing himself from the table, he got up and walked from the room.

He suddenly wasn't hungry for food anymore.

If you enjoyed Destiny's Knight
don't miss the next
Guarded Souls romance

Hope's Wish

David Bowie.

That's all a man needed to decompress.

David Bowie singing "Space Oddity." Add a cold drink to the mix—tonight it was a gin and tonic—and a bowl of pretzels and, in James Hastin's humble opinion, the night could go on forever.

He'd experience more than one night that felt like it would never end during his time in this world. Until Bowie came along, those dragging nights were torturous.

"Why are we at a karaoke bar again?"

Letting a smile curl his lips, James threw the man sitting beside him a sideways look. "I'm feeling generous, Kitt."

Kitt Newton winced, the bar's muted overhead lights flickering in his amber eyes. "I've been told the last time you felt generous, William Shatner was nominated for a Grammy."

James laughed, plucked a pretzel from the

bowl in front of him—a bowl that never emptied, regardless of the fact the barkeeper never topped it up—and tossed it into his mouth.

Pretzels fell into the "good" column.

Salted peanuts, though? Those oily little bastards fell into the "bad" column.

"I'm generous far more often than you realize," he said around a mouthful of crunchy, savory deliciousness. "For instance, Taylor Swift."

Kitt shifted on his stool. James didn't need to look at him to see it. The very air around the other man seemed to growl. "You're telling me you're responsible for Taylor Swift's success?"

Grinning, James threw another pretzel into his mouth and chewed.

Kitt frowned, amber eyes catching the light again, and shook his head. "I never know when to believe you, Hastin."

"I never lie, Rover."

Kitt rolled his eyes and snagged a handful of pretzels himself. "Don't call me Rover." He ate the handful in a single bite and scanned the crowd reflected in the bar's mirrored wall. "So who is it?"

Lifting a just-be-patient finger, James closed his eyes and tasted the longing in the air. Flipped through the silent hopes, dreams, aspirations and desires wafting around him.

So many cravings for sex in the place. So many wishes for an accidental brushing of boob on arm, groin on butt.

So many wishes for a quickie in the alley out back, a tangle in the toilet, a blow job in the backseat of an Uber...

Why an Uber?

Didn't matter. If a blow job in the backseat of an Uber was what the wisher wanted, who was he to point out the impact on their user rating?

After the shit-fire madness he'd just been through helping out Guarded Souls' resident fallen angel, he needed a rush. Needed to tap into an emotional high and wallow about for a bit.

Was the high of oral sex in a moving vehicle the kind of rush he was chasing, though?

"Are you still looking?" Kitt grumbled beside him. "Or have you gone to sleep?"

He smiled, opened his eyes and turned on his stool to face the crowd. "There."

Kitt frowned at the writhing mass of people and took a sip of his Scotch. "Who? Which one? Male or female? Give me a clue, dude."

James smiled. "Patience."

She stood—or rather, fidgeted—on the dance floor a few feet from the unused karaoke stage. She was trying to look like she was dancing, but in her heart of hearts, she was wondering what her date (a firefighter who made her feel special and nervous and safe all at once) would do if she climbed onto the stage and requested the karaoke MC tee up Bon Jovi's "Livin' on a Prayer"?

Let's see, shall we?

James brushed the longing in her heart a little, his blood tingling as she caught her lip with her teeth and flicked a quick glance toward where he and Kitt sat at the bar.

"Ahh." Kitt nodded. "I see. How do you even pick 'em?"

"Trade secret, Rover." He smiled at the woman, dropped her a wink and tossed a pretzel into his mouth.

"I really wish you'd stop calling me that."

James arched an eyebrow. "Do you *really* want to go with that particular choice of words, Kitt?"

"Shit." Kitt held up his hands. "You know that's not what I meant. Stop being so literal." He scowled and pivoted his stool back to the bar. "Remind me again why I hang out with you?"

"Because of this," James said, with another stroke to the woman's longing to sing, to throw caution aside and climbed up onto the stage.

She looked over her shoulder again toward the bar, toward him and Kitt.

Good girl. Good...

With a quick word in her date's ear, she walked over to the bar and rested her elbows on it, right beside James. "Can I get an ice water please?" she asked the barkeeper.

The barkeeper nodded and went to work.

"Thirsty?" James asked, reaching for another pretzel.

She let out a wobbly chuckle and tucked a strand of brown hair behind her ear. "No. Yes. Sorta."

He could feel her heart racing as she gave the stage a glance over her shoulder.

"You going to treat us all to a song?" He danced the pretzel over the back of his knuckles before tossing it into his mouth. "Belt out a tune? I was just saying to Rover here," he clapped a hand on Kitt's shoulder, "I feel a need to hear some Bon Jovi."

Her eyebrows lifted. "'Livin' on a Prayer'?"

"My favorite." He squeezed Kitt's shoulder with a grin. "This one here likes that old song from the '70s, 'Werewolves of London'."

Kitt growled.

The woman chewed her bottom lip again and gave the karaoke stage another glance. James's blood tingled. "I'd love to get up there and sing," she said, as if sharing a profound secret. "But..."

I'm not brave enough. And what if I can't sing it as well as I do in the shower? Her thoughts tickled at James. *And what if my date laughs at—*

"Your water." The barkeeper placed a tall, beading glass in front of her on the bar, and she startled.

"But…?" James prodded. Two words. All he needed to hear were two simple words.

She shrugged and took a sip, studying the stage in the mirrored wall. "I'm not that good. At least, I don't think I am. I wish…"

James smiled. Warmth began to spread through him. His blood didn't just tingle, it rushed through his veins like liquid sunlight mixed with lightning. "You wish what?"

Her eyes met his in the mirror and she caught her bottom lip again. "I wish I was brave enough to not care if I don't sound like Adele, y'know? I wish I could just say to hell with what everyone thinks and go up there and have fun. And I wish, if I did, that I could actually surprise myself and sound amazing."

"Just those three wishes, eh?" James danced another pretzel over his knuckles and winked at her. "I like it. Done."

He nodded his head once—and released the rush.

The woman drew in a swift breath, held it for an eternity, and then slapped her hands on the bar, eyes shining. "Y'know what? To hell with being scared. I'm going to do it!"

"You're going to get up there and sing?" Kitt

asked.

She grinned, slapped the bar again and nodded. "Yep. I'm going to go up there, sing 'Living on a Prayer' and have fun. Who cares, right? I don't." She frowned, as if contemplating what she'd said, and then laughed. "I truly don't!"

With another quick gulp of water, she spun on her heel and almost skipped through the crowd to where her date stood, watching her. Flinging her arms around his neck, she smacked an enthusiastic kiss on his mouth, and then hurried up the ramp to the karaoke MC's station.

"So are you responsible for—" Kitt started, but James silenced him with a finger.

"Shhh, mate," James whispered, riding the tsunami of giddy emotion. "Let me just savor this for a moment."

"Y'know you've lost your American accent, right?"

James didn't care. He closed his eyes, breathed in deeply, and readied himself for the rush of the third wish.

"You sound like a Brit again."

Music began to play, the distinctive introduction of Bon Jovi's seminal '80s classic.

The first word, her first note, hit him. Slammed into him. Flowed through him. Made every molecule in both his solid and ethereal forms frenzied.

The rush of the wish fulfilled.

"Oh yeah." If he still smoked, he'd light up. But it had been almost a thousand years and he wasn't going to start again. "Oh yeah," he repeated on a murmur.

"Yeah." Kitt chuckled, twisting on his stool back to the bar. "I guess that answers the question whether *you're* responsible for her getting up there."

James smiled, eyes still closed.

The woman sang, her voice pure and strong and incredible. Sure, he may have given it a little tweak for the sake of her longing, but she had the natural talent. Would she ever sing karaoke again? He had no clue. That wasn't his concern. Their interaction was done, finished, and he was okay with that.

Another of his kind may have extracted a price, a hidden condition to the covenant before granting her wishes, as he himself had been known to do, but for tonight, for these three wishes...

"You really are feeling generous tonight," Kitt said, a note of approval and awe in his voice.

"Sometimes the world needs a reminder it's not all hell in a handcart." James opened his eyes and watched in the mirror as the woman sang up a storm on the stage. Joy and delight radiated from her, sweetening the rush still flowing through him. On the dance floor stood her date, the musclebound firefighter gazing up at her with the dopiest smile of utter adoration.

James reached for his gin and tonic and held it out to Kitt in a relaxed toast. "To the rush of being a good guy."

Kitt laughed and chinked his glass to James's. "To good guys. Even if few humans know we are."

James winked at the wolf shifter. "Even then."

They grinned and swallowed the rest of their drinks in one go.

"What's with the changing accents?" Kitt asked, wiping at the residue of Scotch on his lips with the back of his hand. "Most of the time you sound British, and occasionally like you're from New Zealand, but I've noticed when you interact with some people, you sound American. And the other day you were talking to someone on the phone and sounded like you were from South Africa. Then a month ago, you were muttering to yourself in the lunch room and sounded Middle Eastern."

James snorted. "Did I? I must have been tired that day."

Kitt lifted an eyebrow.

"When I need to sound American, I sound American. When I need to sound South

African, I sound South African. You see where I'm going with this? My place of origin—I'm talking thousands and thousands and *thousands* of years ago—is the Middle East, so that explains that one, but I spent quite a substantial amount of my existence here amongst mankind in the UK before I moved to LA, so it's sort of become my default accent."

Kitt narrowed his eyes. "There's a lot of secrets going on under that flippant persona of yours, Hastin."

James laughed. "You could say that about every one of us bastards working at Guarded Souls." He moved his attention to the woman now singing Adele's "Rolling in the Deep" on the karaoke stage. She was doing an amazing job, and her date was still gazing at her with rapt attention.

Narrowing his focus on the firefighter's emotions and thoughts, James chuckled. The man was head over heels in love. Her courage to get up and sing had been the final push for his romantic heart.

James closed his eyes, savoring the final waves of the rush. Like the last glimpses of light from the sun as it sank behind the horizon, the final rush flared stronger and more intense, and for a split second he was nothing but elemental force. And then the rush was over. Finished.

Sated, he opened his eyes and let out a long sigh.

"Does it ever piss you off?" Kitt asked. "Not getting any of the credit when you do something like this?" He indicated the singing woman with a slight tilt of his head.

"Something like this…" James smiled. "I do something like this for the rush."

"That good?"

"You have no idea."

Kitt chuckled. "If the expression on your face when she first started to sing was any indication, I think I do. You looked like you were about to blow your load."

James grinned, plucked a pretzel out of thin air and studied its perfection for a second. "Clearly, Rover, you've never seen me just as I'm about to blow my—"

"And I'm eternally grateful for that simple truth," Kitt cut in. "I like you, Genie Boy, but not that much."

"Genie Boy?"

Kitt flashed white teeth at him. "You call me Rover, I call you Genie Boy."

James held aloft his empty glass. "I'll drink to that." It filled to the brim with fresh gin and tonic, at the same moment Kitt's filled with Scotch.

"Ah, now see?" Kitt raised his primed glass. "*This* is why I hang out with you."

"Free booze?"

"Free booze." Kitt tapped his glass to James's. "Cheers."

James laughed. "So, Rover, now I've had my fun, wanna tell me what's the deal with the mysterious text messages you keep getting from—"

James's cellphone vibrated to life in his waistcoat's inside pocket, at the exact moment Kitt's phone did the same on the bar top.

"Message from the boss," Kitt said, frowning at his phone screen even as a wave of relief rolled from him so potent, James felt it. If the text hadn't been from Kade, James would have pushed the issue. Something was troubling the wolf shifter, something dark enough to put him on edge. "He wants us in the office ASAP."

Pulling his own phone from his waistcoat, James read the message on the screen: *Will the wolf and the djinn please get their hairy asses into work pronto? Got an emergency job and I need both of you.*

"Okay, I'll accept your arse is hairy," he said, throwing Kitt a grin, "but mine?"

Kitt snorted, shoving his phone into his pocket as he straightened from the barstool. "Did you drive here?"

"Ah, Rover, you're too adorable for your own hairy-arsed good sometimes." James squeezed Kitt's shoulder. "Ready?"

Kitt's eyes widened. "No. No! Don't you—"

James clicked his fingers.

"—dare," Kitt groaned. He scowled at the Guarded Souls' entry foyer, before turning the scowl on James. "I hate it when you do that."

James grinned. "I know, Rover. I know."

Kitt dragged his hand down his face, shook his head then his shoulders, and let out a ragged breath. "One of these days, I'm going to shift form and cock my leg on—"

"You two took your time." Kade appeared at the door leading into the security firm's offices, his expression as enigmatic as ever. "Hurry up. This is a tricky one."

Without another word, he turned and walked away.

James flicked Kitt a look. "Smell anything fishy?"

"Ha ha." Kitt rolled his eyes, and then drew a slow breath. "Although whoever the tricky client is, she's wearing Chanel No. 5 perfume."

"Why do you know what Chanel No. 5 perfume smells like?"

Kitt dropped him a wink and strode after Kade.

"Fair enough." James followed. Regardless of the fact it was almost midnight, when the boss said it was time to work, it was time to work.

Beyond the quiet entry foyer, Guarded Souls

was silent. Individual offices and meeting rooms sat dark except for Kade's at the end of a wide corridor. White light spilled from the partly opened door, the low murmur of his deep voice rumbling on the air like distant thunder as Kitt stepped into the room.

James threw his own office a quick glance as he walked past. What were the chances his peace lily was still alive? Feathers was probably making certain it was; the angel had a thing for keeping plants going even when water didn't come anywhere near their roots. James himself rarely used the space, with its state-of-the-art office equipment and luxurious, modern furniture, preferring to do any official paperwork either at home or wherever he happened to find himself when it needed to be done.

Plus, there was the fact Nim had foolishly said to him she'd do anything for a Reuben sandwich, and he'd granted her wish. The wiccan was now doing his paperwork for a month. (She really did need to rethink how loosely she threw the W-word around in the lunchroom.)

As far as work went, being on the Guarded Souls payroll was pretty cushy; most of the clients engaging the agency's protection and security services were extremely rich and, in the majority of cases, more paranoid about being under threat than they were any kind of actual target. But it did make for some interesting work hours. Not really a problem for James—or any of those employed by Kade. Given that none of the protection staff were human, common human hours weren't an issue. But the ancient vampire did like to maintain a human façade for the firm, which meant keeping normal business hours for the ancillary staff.

Being called in for a job at midnight, though? That was…different.

Even more different? Kade using the term *tricky*.

In the years that James had been a Guarded Souls member, he'd only ever seen Kade stressed once. And that was when the entire security team, including Kade himself, almost—

"…getting tired of being treated like a fragile victim here."

James froze at the female voice coming from Kade's office. His heart smashed up into his throat.

Fark.

He knew that voice, that Northern English accent. That fierce confidence.

It's not her. Can't be. She's in London. You know that. She's—

"Because I'm not," the woman went on, the calm challenge in her voice more familiar than his own reflection. "Fragile. Or a victim. I merely heard something I wasn't meant to."

Yep. It was her.

Shite. Why in the name of all things British was Tahlee Hope here in LA?

Bracing himself for what was about to happen, James stepped into Kade's office and smiled at the woman he'd left three years ago. "Hey, Hope. Long time no speak to."

More Romance from Lexxie Couper...

Fire Mates Series

Sera's Dragon
How to Love Your Dragon
Tigress and the Dragon
Scorched Desire

And many more

About Lexxie Couper

Lexxie Couper started writing when she was six and hasn't stopped since. She's not a deviant, but she does have a deviant's imagination and a desire to entertain readers with her words. Add the two together and you get erotic romances that can make you laugh, cry, shake with fear or tremble with desire. Sometimes all at once.

When she's not submerged in the worlds she creates, Lexxie's life revolves around her family, a husband who thinks she's insane, a indoor cat who likes to stalk shadows, and her daughters, who both utterly captured her heart and changed her life forever.

Lexxie lives by two simple rules – measure your success not by how much money you have, but by how often you laugh, and always try everything at least once. As a consequence, she's laughed her way through many an eyebrow raising adventure.

You can find details of her writing at
www.LexxieCouper.com